The Sweater's Punishment

or

The Champion of the Oppressed

By G. H. Teed

Illustrated by Val Reading

First published in The Union Jack magazine,
3 October 1914, Series 2 No. 573.

Stillwoods Edition

Stillwoods.Blogspot.Ca

Catalogue Information:
Title: The Sweater's Punishment
Sub-Title: The Champion of the Oppressed
Author: G. H. Teed (1881-1938)
Illustrated by: Val Reading
First published anonymously in The Union Jack magazine, 3 October 1914, Series 2 No. 573.
This Edition by: Stillwoods, 2021
ISBN Canada: 978-1-989788-82-0
Blog: Stillwoods.Blogspot.Ca
Author Blog: http://ghteed.blogspot.com/
Storefront: http://www.lulu.com/spotlight/lulubook22

https://tinyurl.com/ve25d42s This link should go to a spreadsheet of all known Teed stories. The list is annotated with various information on the stories and my progress with recapturing the work. The library of Teed's stories increases almost weekly. Check at the **Lulu.Com** for the latest arrivals. Search for Teed./drf

Keywords: Sexton Blake, British fictional detective, Tinker, Yvonne Cartier

Cautionary Note: This series of books by Stillwoods are intended to make the stories of G. H. Teed, born in New Brunswick, Canada, available to collectors and researchers. The editor, or rather digitizer has not altered the original publication.

This story may contain language and racial terms that are not appropriate to today. I apologize for them; I know that the author was using his voice to excite and entertain an adventurous English audience. These works were published from 82 to 110 years ago. Most every work has characters of redeeming ethnicity within.

I hope you enjoy and share these stories; I have.
Doug Frizzle

The Return of Yvonne! A Long Yarn, introducing Mdlle. YVONNE, SEXTON BLAKE, Etc., etc.

THE SWEATER'S PUNISHMENT

OR,

The Champion of the Oppressed.

A Long Yarn, introducing Mdlle. YVONNE, SEXTON BLAKE, etc., etc.

(Illustrated by "VAL.")

Sexton Blake . . . . . walked slowly into the room.

Through a traffic accident, Yvonne becomes angry at employment practises in London. Sexton Blake is soon dragged into a series of crimes, and Yvonne is suspected.

At Queen Anne's Gate a massive plum-coloured car drew away from the kerb. Inside, the rays from the tiny electric light fell on the sumptuous fittings, revealing them in a dully gleaming array of richness. From the ivory-mounted toilet articles in their plum-coloured case, to the soft upholstery of the seat, it spoke of wealth and good taste.

In front sat the driver, as perfectly mechanical in his movements as the car itself. But if the car and its liveried chauffeur were products of modem perfection, the girl who leaned back against the soft cushions inside was no less exquisite example of the costumier's art.

She was gowned in pale, filmy blue, which fell about her slim figure in long, graceful folds. From beneath peeped the toe of a tiny satin slipper of the same delicate shade, revealing the barest hint of a silk-clad ankle. Over her shoulders was thrown a rich evening wrap of silver-grey, open at the throat, and permitting the rays of the light to fall on a great diamond drop which blazed against the white throat.

Resting on a base of coiled and twisted bronze hair was a fragile tiara embedded with diamonds which shot forth scintillating shafts of blue and green and red as the car swayed gently. It was a perfect setting to the chaste beauty of the girl herself, for the girl was Yvonne.

From Queen Anne's Gate the car made its way towards Oxford Street, leading for Shaftesbury Avenue. It was still early in the evening, barely seven, yet already the lights were twinkling throughout the streets, tribute to the approach of autumn.

Alec, who was driving, picked his way along slowly, knowing that his mistress was a little early for her engagement. Yvonne, lost in reverie, and giving no thought to the dinner party for which she was bound, lay back with closed eyes.

From Oxford Street Alec turned into Shaftesbury Avenue, and drove carefully through the heavy theatre traffic which already filled it. Half way along he stopped with a jerk, and leaned forward tensely. From far ahead came shouts and cries laden with something out of the ordinary.

Suddenly vehicles began dashing in every direction, leaving an open lane down which thundered a great dray drawn by four maddened horses which were running wild. Still clinging to the reins was the driver, drawn along at their heels with sickening thuds and bumps. In a few moments they must be upon him.

He looked round hastily. One swift glance told him it would be impossible to back up. A chaotic mass of vehicles were jammed together in a frenzied effort to get clear. He sized up his chances with a practised eye. If the dray continued its present course, nothing could save the car.

Turning, he rapped on the window behind him. Yvonne came out of her reverie, and raised herself with a jerk. Instinctively she reached for the telephone.

"What is it, Alec?" she asked quickly.

"Runaway, mademoiselle, jump out quick! I'll try to save the car."

"I'll stick, Alec. Can you make the side street just ahead?"

"I might, but I'll have to go over the footpath to do it, It's our only chance. Hang on when she bumps!"

While Alec threw in the clutch and sent the car ahead with a terrific jump, Yvonne clung to the arm straps and watched. A few yards on was the small side street which was their objective. Beyond it and thundering towards them was the dray.

To make the street and turn into it in the ordinary way was impossible. As Alec had said, their only chance was to cut over the footpath. Had it not been for a sloping section which dropped flush with the road, even that chance would have been denied them.

While the car still gathered way, Alec turned it towards the spot, tooting his horn frantically to warn the few pedestrians who had not already found shelter. There was a violent lurch as the front wheels struck it, then Alec gave another sharp twist to the steering-wheel, which almost threw Yvonne to the floor.

Along the pavement it dashed until the corner was reached. There was no time now to continue to the road itself. Their only hope was to risk turning the corner on the footpath, and taking the side street over the high kerb.

Nearer and nearer drew the four crazed horses, until it seemed to Yvonne that they must come crashing into them. Then there was a terrific bumping and lurching as Alec left the footpath and took the road.

Scarcely had he done so when the dray swept past. A wild shriek followed, accompanied by a splintering noise as horses and dray crashed into a taxi which was endeavouring to escape.

But Yvonne's attention was suddenly brought back from the rear window of the car. Like an echo of the cry the taxi-driver had given, a scream sounded in front. The grinding of the brakes followed, and the car slewed sharply as Alec brought it to a standstill.

Yvonne saw him jump from his place, saw a policeman run across to them, saw a crowd begin to gather, then she raised herself and stepped out. A glance showed her what had happened. In avoiding the danger of the greater street, they had done so at the cost of a pedestrian in the smaller street.

Huddled up against the front wheel was a dark bundle which Alec and the policeman were extricating with difficulty. In front of the car, to the side and stretching clear to the kerb, were pools and streams of vivid purple which, on closer examination, Yvonne found to be heaps upon heaps of tiny artificial blossoms of silk. In the gutter lay a large basket, crushed and broken, from which the blossoms had fallen.

Turning, she found that Alec and the policeman had lifted the crumpled bundle out from beneath the car. Her eyes fell on a white, haggard face, lined and seamed with trouble and sorrow. It was the face of a woman prematurely aged, and when she gazed upon the frail, twisted body, garbed in cheap black, Yvonne saw the frailty born of starvation.

Swiftly she dropped to her knees, reckless of her rich gown, and, taking the woman's head in her lap, motioned imperatively for Alec to bring a flask of spirits from the car. When a little had been poured between the pinched lips, the woman opened her eyes and gazed about her vaguely. Then her glance fell upon the scattered blossoms, and she gave a sobbing cry.

"My flowers, my flowers!" she whispered. "Oh, what will they say?"

"Don't worry about the flowers," answered Yvonne soothingly. "I will arrange about them all right. You have been knocked down by my car, and I am going to take you home. Then we will have a doctor, and find out if you have been injured. Come now, be brave! We are going to lift you into the car."

Yvonne held the woman's hand, while Alec and the constable lifted her into the car and laid her on the soft cushions; then she bent forward.

"Tell me," she said, "where do you live?"

"A long distance," whispered the woman. "Greig Street, No. 20."

Yvonne gave the address to Alec, then, satisfying the constable with the particulars he desired, stepped in and sunk down beside the other. Alec climbed into his place, and once more the car started for the East End of the city, leaving behind the tumbled heap of purple blossoms.

Winding and twisting in and out of a series of narrow, choked streets, the car finally came to a stop before a high, dark tenement in a particularly noisome and odorous street.

Almost before Alec had opened the door a bevy of dirty urchins was gathered about, making audible remarks about Yvonne and her gown. Brushing them aside, Alec helped out his mistress, then commandeered the services of a sodden-looking individual who at that moment lounged out of the door of the tenement.

Between them they got the woman into the building, and at her direction opened a rickety door on the ground floor. They carried her into a meagrely furnished room littered with silk and tiny strands of wire.

At a long table sat five pinched, starved-looking children, ranging in age from seven to fifteen. Before them were bits of the silk and wire at which they worked feverishly, making blossoms similar to those Yvonne had seen back in the street.

The two elder, a scraggy boy and frail girl, dropped their work and sprang forward as the little party entered. The three younger children burst into sobs and whimpered pitifully. Yvonne swept the room with her eyes and, noticing a dilapidated couch at one side, motioned to Alec to lay the woman upon it.

Then she turned to him:

"Alec, give this man who has helped you half-a-crown. If he will remain within call for a little, he shall receive another. You take the car and bring Dr. Gordon.

"Then make these purchases. Buy two cooked chickens, bread, milk, tea, coffee, some port wine for this poor woman, cakes and pastries, and anything else you see that you think would be nice. Hurry back with them. And, by the way, send a telegram to Major Gilbert's that I shall not be there for dinner. I shall remain here until you return."

As Alec hurried away, taking the shabby individual, Yvonne

turned back to the children and began to soothe them. When their fright had subsided somewhat, she drew up a chair beside the white-faced woman and took one thin hand between her own firm young fingers.

"Tell me," she said softly, "do you feel any pain?"

"No, miss, not much. My leg hurts a little, but I don't think any bones are broken."

"I can't tell you how terribly sorry I am," went on Yvonne. "You see, it was while we were trying to save ourselves from the runaway that we struck you."

"I know, miss. You have been very kind. There's those what strike a poor body down and drive on without taking the trouble to see what has happened. But nobody could do more than you have done. Only—only—"

"Only what!" prompted Yvonne.

"My flowers—a whole week's work gone, and the blossoms ruined. Oh, what they will say I don't know!"

"Who is it to whom you refer?" asked Yvonne.

"The factory what gives me the work to do, miss. I was taking them there when I was struck."

"And is that how you and your children live—by making artificial flowers?"

"Yes, miss, like you see on the table."

Yvonne rose, and picking up one of the blossoms examined it.

"In the West End one would pay anything from ten shillings to thirty shillings for one of these" she mused. Then aloud:

"They are very beautiful indeed. I suppose you got a very fair price for them?"

"Ninepence a dozen, miss,"

"Ninepence a— Oh, say that again!"

"Ninepence a dozen, miss."

Yvonne's eyes held a curious gleam in them when she spoke again.

"How many do you make in a day?"

"I make a dozen and a half, and the two elder children do another dozen between them. That makes two dozen and a half a day. The younger children cut the silk and wire into the proper lengths."

"And how long each day do you work?"

"We begin at daylight, miss. The children stop at nine, but I usually go on until midnight."

"That means that, working from daylight to midnight you earn, with the help of your five children, something like one shilling and tenpence halfpenny a day. Do you work Sunday?"

"I do, miss. The children go to the Mission Sunday-school."

"In a week's time your earnings total about—twelve shillings?"

"Yes, miss."

"How much do you pay for rent?"

"Four shillings a week, and we have a good landlord. When the youngest child was ill last winter, he waited six weeks for his money."

"That leaves you eight shillings a week on which to support yourself and five children?"

"Yes, miss."

"How do you do it? What do you eat?"

"Usually bread and dripping with a little piece of meat on Sundays. We manage fairly well."

"Bread and dripping with a little piece of meat on Sundays, and she manages fairly well!" repeated Yvonne in an odd tone. "Have you a husband?"

"Yes, miss," answered the woman in a low tone. "He is in prison. He has been away two years."

Yvonne sat down again.

"What is the name of the man who pays you to do this work?" she asked.

"Sir Hector Trott, miss. He has a large factory. There are a good many out-hands."

"Sir Hector Trott!"

Yvonne was silent, remembering that only that morning she had read two items in her paper about Sir Hector Trott. One was that he had given a thousand pounds to an orphanage, and that the Press had acclaimed him as the well-known philanthropist.

The other item was a paragraph saying that Sir Hector had purchased the famous horse, "Sunset," which he intended sending to the stud at his country place. The price mentioned was twenty thousand pounds.

"I think you said there were a good many out-workers. Do they all do this work?"

"Just now we are all on it, miss. The foreman said we must get in all we could, as they had a contract for a thousand dozen of them."

"How much do the others make out at it?"

"Some as well as I do, miss, but most are worse off. You see some has worthless husbands and some no children to help."

"I am going to give you five pounds before I go," said Yvonne quietly. "out of that you can pay the foreman for the ruined blossoms. Then, I am coming to see you often. By the way, what is your name?"

"Harrison, Miss."

"Well, Mrs. Harrison, I don't want you to worry. Send word to the factory that you will not be able to do any work for a few days at least, if they send for the stuff, and refuse to let you continue, don't worry. In the meantime, I shall take care of you until I plan something for you. Now I hear the car outside. It is probably the doctor."

A moment later the door opened and a brisk looking young man entered. He greeted Yvonne with surprise.

"I couldn't imagine why you had sent for me to come into this part. Your man told me nothing."

Yvonne gave him her hand.

"We knocked down this poor woman. I want you to examine her and tell me what she needs. My car was responsible, so I want to take care of her."

"I'll run over her in a few moments," he replied.

As he opened his bag and went to work, Yvonne moved into the adjoining room to see for herself what kind of a bed-room the family had. It was a pitiful sight, and her heart contracted with the pain of knowledge as she gazed upon it.

Outside the doctor was busy, nor did poor Mrs. Harrison dream that she was being attended by one of the crack Harley Street men, whose fee for a single visit was usually more than she would earn in many months.

He called to Yvonne when he had finished. She came out at once and followed him to the opposite side of the room.

"Nothing serious," he said in a low tone. "A little shock, and a few bruises. She needs rest and quiet, but there is something else she needs more."

"You mean?"

"Food! It must be ages since she has had a proper meal. The woman is actually dying from lack of nourishment and overwork. And, unfortunately, there are more in these slums like her than unlike her."

"It is terrible, doctor. But I intend looking after her, and getting some different work for her. If she will go, I will send her to the country."

"If some of the charitable organisations would spend more money in doing that and less in pamphlets for soul food, the slums would be saner and better," he said brusquely. "But, I must be going. I have to run in and visit Sir Hector Trott his evening."

Yvonne gave a start at the coincidence.

"Sir Hector Trott!" she echoed. "Is he ill?"

Doctor Gordon smiled.

"No! He sends for me every little while. I suppose he has just been overeating."

Yvonne's lips curled as she thought of the contrast; then she said: "What will be the fee for this call, doctor? I will pay you now."

He held up his hand.

"Not a penny. I think I can afford a charitable visit occasionally. Heaven knows, it is not because I don't wish to that I don't make more. I will receive enough from Sir Hector Trott to pay me for both visits. And now good night. If you need me again, let me know and I will come."

Soon after Alec returned, bringing with him all the articles of food which his mistress had mentioned as well as a variety of things he himself had thought of. Alec knew from the hard experience of his younger days what would be most welcome in the slums.

As he piled the great heap of parcels on the table, Yvonne called to the children to help. To the accompaniment of many "Ohs!" and "Ahs!" their nimble fingers undid the dainties, and then there followed such a feast in that poor tenement room as they had never dreamed of.

Yvonne prepared things with her own hands while Alec handed round the heaping piles. Then when the remains had been put away for the morrow, Yvonne and the children cleaned up. That finished, Yvonne put Mrs. Harrison to bed while the older children prepared the younger ones for their cots.

And so the little weary eyes closed drowsily as they went off into Dreamland, led through wonderful green fields by the hand of a dazzling fairy dressed in shimmering blue.

Promising to return on the morrow Yvonne left some money with

Mrs. Harrison, and silencing the grateful woman's outpourings of thanks with her soft hand, went out. Getting into the car she turned off the light, and through the telephone told Alec to drive into the country.

Then the big car started, and soon after was spinning along past the open fields. On and on it went with the faithful Alec bending over the wheel. Inside Yvonne lay back in the corner thinking, thinking, thinking.

For a startling idea had come into her mind; an idea which if pursued would mean a radical change in her present mode of living. It would mean the severing of many ties, and she knew one tie in particular that she would be in danger of cutting.

Yet what she had seen that night had made a tremendous impression upon her. Had it not been for one thing she would have decided immediately. But that one thing was— Blake. Could she give up the friendship which meant so much to her? For she realised that it would have to be given up.

At that moment her hand fell on one of the purple blossoms which she had absent-mindedly brought with her. She picked it up, and as it brought back vividly all she had seen and heard, she decided.

With a little choking sob she leaned back, murmuring brokenly:

"It won't make any difference. His work is everything to him."

Then her eyes closed, and only the clenched hands told she was suffering. And when the great plum-coloured car finally drew up again in front of her house at Queen Anne's Gate, the chill dawn was mantling the east.

Not heeding her fine gown, Yvonne knelt down in the road beside the old woman, and raised the flask to her lips.

GRAVES was idling over his breakfast when Yvonne appeared. To look at her in her fresh white morning dress one could hardly believe that she had been riding about in the car until daylight. Her uncle's remark proved that he for one knew nothing of it.

"Good morning, Yvonne! You look as fresh as a daisy. I didn't see you when I came in. Did you retire early?"

"I didn't get in until five o'clock, uncle," she answered, as she seated herself.

"Didn't get in until five! Good heavens! did they dance all night at the Gilberts?"

"I didn't go—not even to dinner."

"I don't think I understand, Yvonne. You left here to go there."

"I know, but something occurred on the way which caused me not to. By the way, uncle, what do you know about conditions in the slums?"

Graves shrugged.

"What everyone knows—that they are a growing sore in the side of Society."

"Did it ever occur to you that Society itself may be the cause of it?"

"My dear Yvonne, why this at the breakfast table? Are you thinking of taking up social work? Because if you are, let me give you one word of advice."

"What is that?"

"Don't! Generations of workers have tried to change conditions there. In all great cities it is the same. And as long as society is organised as it is, it must remain so. One man—a hundred men—can do nothing. Millions have been poured in; and it is impossible to see any effect.

"Many good men and women are working there now. In twenty years they will see no result for their work. A solitary case here and there may be held up as a conquest—a soul saved. But for that one a thousand have gone under."

"Society may be the cause of it, but society has tried to cure it. It is like the grotesque creature of a man's brain which has risen up and dominated him who gave it being. To fight the evil as it is being fought is like treating an infectious disease by absent treatment."

11

"But is society really trying to cure it, uncle?"

"They say so," responded Graves cynically. "But what is your motive in this, Yvonne?"

Briefly she related what had happened the previous night, telling him also how she had pondered during the long ride.

"I feel as you do, uncle, that individual effort counts for little, but I think if some of those who caused wholesale suffering were to suffer themselves, it would attract attention to their cases, and for very shame they must stop their terrible sweating practices.

"At any rate I have quite made up my mind to try the experiment. I realise all it means giving up. It means leaving here, and once more taking up a precarious life; for my methods will not be the methods as approved by the law."

"What do you mean, Yvonne?" asked Graves with quick concern.

"I mean, I intend wielding the rod of punishment against some of the worst offenders, and the first one to receive my attention is going to be Sir Hector Trott,"

"What method will you adopt?"

"Do you remember how I avenged my mother's death, uncle?"

"Can I ever forget? But do you mean to say you intend following that line?"

"Yes, and let me say, uncle, that I do not expect you to join me. You are happy here in London with your clubs and your friends, I should neither expect it nor ask it."

"Tut-tut, Yvonne. Have you thought over carefully every point?"

"Yes!"

"Even to the likelihood of your being once more on opposite sides to a certain individual?"

"Yes," whispered Yvonne.

"And still you are determined?"

"Yes!"

"Then I suppose you will do as you say. Personally, I regret your decision exceedingly. I have been happy here, as you say, but if you leave I shall go too. You are as dear to me as my own daughter. If you must do these quixotic things my place is with you. You are all I have. I am all you have. Still, I am sorry."

Yvonne left her place and knelt beside him.

"Dear uncle," she said; "I feel a beast, but I can't alter my decision. Were things different I should gladly do so. But I am weary

12

of it all, and, now that I have a motive, I feel that I must pursue it until I succeed or fail."

"What will Blake say?"

"He has his work," she replied, in muffled tones.

"He thinks too much of his work," said Graves savagely.

"But, come, Yvonne, if you must do this thing, tell me what your plans are."

"I have decided nothing definite yet, uncle. But to-day we will leave here. We shall motor to Yarmouth where the yacht is lying. Then I will call all hands together. Each can decide for himself if he wishes to stay. Those who don't care to run any risk will be free to leave."

"They will stay all right," grunted Graves. "There isn't a man on the Fleur-de-Lys who wouldn't follow you through anything. They will probably hail your proposal with delight. What time do we start?"

"As soon as we can get ready. Anna is packing now. I have a call to make first, then a letter to write, and I shall be ready. We can probably get away about four."

Graves rose a trifle wearily, and went to see about his packing. He was not as young and care-free as be used to be, and it would be a considerable tug to cut all his old ties. But he loved the strange, wayward girl with all his warm nature, and existence without Yvonne was unthinkable.

As for Yvonne she barely touched the dainty breakfast, and shortly followed her uncle from the room. She motored through to Greig Street, as she had promised, and spent an hour with Mrs. Harrison. Before she left she had engaged a neighbour in the tenement to look after her, and, leaving sufficient money to run things until she could come again, drove back to Queen Anne's Gate.

Anna, the maid, had worked valiantly, and already the luggage was piled up in the hall ready to go. Hastening to the den at the end of the hall, Yvonne seated herself at the desk, and began to write. When she had finished her letter she addressed an envelope, and sent it at once to be posted.

Then they got away, leaving Anna to follow with the luggage. They drove straight to Yarmouth, and just about the time they were going aboard the Fleur-de-Lys that night Sexton Blake in his apartment at Baker Street was opening a letter.

When he first saw the writing on the envelope a pleasurable sense of anticipation had filled him, but, as he grasped the contents, the look faded to give place to one of consternation. For this is what he read:

"My dear comrade,—For probably the last time I am calling you that. I am going away, and, by the time you receive this, I shall have gone. Don't think I have taken the present step without considering all the elements involved. I have done so, and I think you know how the severing of some ties has hurt. But it must be. To go on as I have gone on is impossible, at least for the present. I am young enough to feel impatient with Fate, and it is impossible to resign myself to the contemplation of the happiness of others while I sit alone. There has been so much truth between us a little more can't hurt. At the same time I would not let you see in my heart as I am doing if I were remaining. But why should the chief fact be submerged to trumpery conventions? Had it not been that your work was paramount to you, perhaps you might have seen beyond it. But now it is good-bye! I shall try to forget you, yet always will you live in my memory as a dear friend and comrade. If we ever meet again it may be on opposite sides in the struggle —as first we met. Knowing you as I do, I know your duty must be done. Nor would I have it otherwise. Again, good-by! Perhaps you will think a little from time to time of

"YVONNE."

"P.S.—Tell Tinker I think of him as I leave, and give dear old Pedro a big hug for me.

"Y."

Blake's eyes raced over the last words, then he leaped to his feet. Glancing at the clock, he saw that it was just twelve minutes to nine. Had she gone yet? Or was there a chance of catching her?

Only too well he read the meaning of the brief phrases in that letter. But it must not be. If any persuasion of his could stop her, he must use it. He bent to the telephone, and asked for her number. Impatiently he waited while the girl tried to get the connection. Ominously her voice came over the wire to him. "They don't answer."

He hung up the receiver, and looked round for his hat. Remembering that he had left it in the dressing-room, he pushed open the door, and caught it up. Rushing through the consulting room he made for the street.

He hailed a crawling taxi.

"Queen Anne's Gate. A sovereign if you get there before nine."

14

The man nodded, and, while the door was yet swinging closed, started off with a jerk. While they lurched and swayed onwards Blake lay back, a prey to his thoughts.

What had happened to cause her to take such a step? Only two days ago he had seen her, and she had seemed perfectly contented. Was it possible that beneath a smiling face she had carried a continual ache? What had she meant by saying if they met again in the future it might be on opposite sides? Why had she said she was going to try to forget him?

And there, in that rocking taxi, Sexton Blake realised with compelling force that he did not want her to forget him. Nor did he want her to go out of his life. He set his jaw grimly and leaned forward as though to make the cab go still faster.

At last they turned into Queen Anne's Gate, and almost before the driver had jerked it to a standstill, Blake was out calling; "Wait!" as he dashed across the pavement and up the steps. Reaching the hall, he hurried to the door of Yvonne's great flat.

He rang and waited; then rang again. No answer. Only the muffled sound of the bell could be heard echoing mockingly in a silent house. At that moment the janitor appeared, and Blake called him.

"Do you know if the tenants of this flat are gone?" he asked.

"Yes, sir. They went this afternoon."

"Have you any idea where they went?"

"No, sir. The lady said they would leave no address as they would probably be gone for months."

"Didn't they leave a servant to look after the place?"

"No, sir. I have promised to look in once a week to see that things are all right."

Blake tossed the man half-a-crown, and made his way slowly to the street. Just as he reached it a neighbouring church clock boomed out the hour of nine as though sounding the knell on his hopes.

"Baker Street," he said wearily, and re-entering the taxi, closed his eyes.

The next morning Blake read in his paper that the yacht, Fleur-de-Lys, having the owner on board, had sailed from Yarmouth.

End of Prologue.

"Miss Craig," the new typist, at Trott's.

THE STORY.

THE Trott Manufacturing Company was one of the largest manufacturing establishments in England. From a small building it had grown, in twenty years, to be a great pile of many floors, employing several hundreds of hands.

To a business of such magnitude the employment or dismissal a typist was a matter of small moment. Amongst the score of girls who sat before the typing machines in the great office one was but a unit, and so perfectly organised was the office end of the business, that, when a vacancy occurred, it was smoothly overlapped by the other employees until it had been filled again.

Yet even so, the manager, who sat in the sumptuous private office and ran things so successfully, had already marked out a typist who had been with the firm scarcely three weeks. She had come with the most excellent credentials and had slipped into the swing of things with exceptional ease and competency.

By chance the manager had one day requested her to take some dictation, and, pleased by her rapidity and the neatness of the finished work, he had appropriated her for his own correspondence.

On a certain Monday morning she was sitting beside him taking down the rapid dictation which he jerked out as he opened his letters and tossed them into a basket. But, when she had finished and astonished him by informing him that she was sorry, but she must ask him to accept a weeks notice, he certainly did not connect it with any of his dictation that morning.

Yet it was a fact, and the following short letter had been the cause. It was in reply to a query from Jarridge's, the great retail establishment in the West End, asking when the Trott Manufacturing Company would be able to deliver their order for one thousand dozen silk blossoms.

Morris, the manager, had dictated an answer at once which ran thus:

"Dear Sirs,—In reply to your inquiry regarding your esteemed order for one thousand dozen artificial blossoms, we beg to advise you that this order will be delivered one week from date.

"Trusting this will be satisfactory and soliciting further of your esteemed orders.

"We beg to remain, etc.,

"Trott Manufacturing Co."

Then he had gone ahead with the rest of his correspondence, totally unaware that the bronze head bent so close to him concealed a pair of flashing blue eyes. Consequently when the typist rose and requested to be relieved of her duties in a week's time, the manager stared.

"What's the matter, Miss Craig? Aren't you satisfied?"

"Perfectly, Mr. Morris. Only it is necessary for me to leave in a week's time."

"But there must be some reason, you have only been here three weeks. I don't mind saying that I have been most pleased with your work. If it is a question of salary, perhaps I could—"

"It is not that, Mr. Morris. It is a question of my own affairs. They make it necessary for me to leave."

"Then you will not stay after Saturday?

"Very well, Miss Craig. If you change your mind, let me know. Get those letters done at once, please. I want to give you some more."

"Miss Craig" passed out to her desk, leaving the manager in a very ill-humour.

"Always the way," he muttered chewing at a cigar. "Find a clever girl, and she no sooner gets the hang of things than she leaves. Going to get married probably."

With that he dismissed the subject from his mind, and returned to his work. His next move was to press a button in his desk. To the boy who answered it he said:

"Find the foreman, and send him here at once."

Ten minutes later the foreman put in an appearance.

"Come here, Johns," said the manager. "I want to talk to you."

When the other was standing beside the desk, the manager went on.

"How about that flower order for Jarridge's? When will it be finished?"

"About ten days yet, Mr. Morris."

"It must be done sooner, Johns. I have had a letter from Jarridge's this morning. They are getting impatient. You know we had a hard job breaking in there, and our future business with them hangs on this order."

"I know that, sir, and I am rushing things as fast as possible."

"All the blooms are being made by out-workers, aren't they?"

"Yes, sir."

"Let's see, we are paying ninepence a dozen, and supplying the silk and wire?"

"Yes, sir."

"Well, things must be speeded up, Johns. I'll tell you what to do. Cut down the price to eightpence a dozen. The extra penny means a lot to those people. They won't want to lose it, and in order to make as much as they are making now they will turn out more. Half-a-dozen extra per day from each worker should get the order completed."

"It would, sir, but have you considered how little those out-workers are getting as it is? They earn barely enough to keep body and soul together, Mr. Morris. I know for a fact that many of them are working from dawn to midnight."

"I can't help that, Johns!" snapped the manager. "There is no sentiment in business. We are out against competition. I want that order completed by Saturday. If the present out-workers don't speed up take the work away from them and get others who will. We are not a philanthropic organisation. Remember, get that order completed by Saturday. That is all."

As the foreman turned slowly away the manager, for the first time, became aware that Miss Craig was standing at the other side of his desk, holding a batch of letters ready for his signature.

So the week rushed by. As he had begun it, so did Morris, the manager, finish it—domineering, driving, and ruthlessly demanding.

Not that he was what the world calls a hard man, nor was he any villain of melodrama. He was merely a man whose sentiments had been crushed under the force of big business.

He had gained the high position he held by sheer ability to get results, and he held it by still continuing this policy. He was what is called a valuable citizen, and, had anyone told him that he was a party to one of the most iniquitous systems of sweating, he would have laughed in disbelief.

He had heard of the slums, and had a vague idea that there were many organisations which tended to alleviate the suffering there. He contributed more modestly to the charitable lists which Sir Hector Trott's name headed, and rested easy in his conscience that he gave his share to the poor and suffering. Perhaps he did by the world's standards.

Had he ever taken the trouble to visit many of the terrible homes in which some of the daintiest output of the firm was made, he might have been brought to a realisation of the truth. But he was too busy to follow what he considered a sentimental fancy, and failed to understand his foreman's point of view.

That the out-workers toiled for a mere pittance compared to the profit the factory made on the output did not worry him. He paid the prices which others paid, and that was all he could be expected to do. Did he pay more and present to the directors a statement showing reduced profits he would soon be looking for another place.

In the City, more than any place else, it is a case of the survival of the fittest. And in big businesses the man who gets the biggest results, no matter what the cost in human strength, is the man who picks the plums.

And on the following Saturday the manager's ability to get things done was proved. Early in the morning Johns, the foreman, came to him and reported that the last dozen the Jarridge order had been brought in. Things had gone pretty well during the week, and, as a consequence, Morris was in a good humour.

He genially informed the foreman that he himself would come down to inspect the blossoms, and, telling Miss Craig to whom he had been dictating, that he would be back in a few minutes, he passed out.

Now, in the ordinary course of events, Miss Craig would have left the room, too, and gone to work on the dictation she had taken until he had again sent for her. But she was very leisurely in rising, and even more leisurely in gathering up her things. Consequently, Morris and the foreman were already out of the room before she had even turned from the desk.

Instead of following them she stood perfectly still for a few minutes until she heard a distant door slam, then she began to act with a swiftness strangely at variance with her former leisurely manner.

Laying her shorthand book and pencil back on the desk she thrust her fingers inside her blouse and drew out a small leather bag, which was suspended from her neck by a chain. Loosening the mouth of it she took out a piece of wax. With this in her hand she stood listening again, then hastily bent over the desk.

In the top drawer dangled a bunch of keys left there by the manager when he had unlocked the drawer. There were perhaps half a dozen on the ring, but only two of these appeared to be of interest to

"Miss Craig."

One was large—so large, in fact, that, when she took an impression of it in the wax, it was only possible to get half of it. But that half was not the half which was attached to the ring. It was the half which formed the business end of the key.

The other which attracted her attention was a small Yale key. Of this she got a complete impression. Then, examining both keys in order to see that there was no particle of wax adhering to them, she returned the lump to the little leather bag and pushed it back beneath her blouse. That done she turned calmly and picked up her books, tripping out of the office with an odd little smile hovering on her lips.

A few minutes later, when the manager had returned from his inspection of the blossoms for the Jarridge order, he sent for Miss Craig, and completed his dictation. Then he rose, and, after locking his desk, put his keys in his pocket.

"I am going now, Miss Craig. I shall probably not be back until the afternoon, and by then you will have gone. Before I go I should like to say that if you change your mind let me know, and I will find a vacancy for you."

"Thank you, Mr. Morris, but I don't think I shall change my mind."

"Very well. When you finish those letters leave them on the desk in here. I will sign them when I return."

Picking up his hat he passed out, and this time "Miss Craig." followed him at once. When one o'clock came work ceased in the great factory until Monday morning.

At five minutes to one "Miss Craig" placed on the desk of the manager all the letters she had done. At two minutes to one she shook hands with her fellow-typists, and bade them good-bye. At one o'clock she presented herself at the cashier's window and received the little envelope containing her week's wages. At three minutes past one she was in the street jostling her way through the crowds.

A few blocks on she came to an old church tucked away in the heart of the business district—a church which she knew was an inseparable part of the district. Outside the door was a box bearing the inscription; "For the Poor."

"Miss Craig" approached it, and, tearing open the envelope containing her week's wages, Stuffed every penny through the slit in the box. Then she tossed the envelope away.

"There goes the last of Miss Craig," she murmured, as she went on her way. "Now I can be Yvonne again, and, unless I am greatly mistaken, the Trott Manufacturing Company will regret that they ever had Miss Craig in their employ. Although they sha'n't know that—if I can prevent it."

She walked on steadily until she came to the Bank. There a big touring car was drawn up at the kerb as though awaiting its owner. In the front seat sat the driver, and those who knew Yvonne would have known that he wore her livery. She paused beside it long enough to say; "Home, Alec!" Then she entered the tonneau and leaned back.

Slowly the car moved ahead into the traffic, but when Alec had brought it into a less congested thoroughfare he sent it along at a good pace. Straight through the City they drove, and on past the suburbs until the open country was reached. Then the pace was increased still more as they raced along the road to Surrey.

None but the members of Yvonne's "circle" knew that the departure of the Fleur-de-Lys from Yarmouth had been more or less of a bluff in case future developments should attract attention to her. Once at sea Yvonne had called hands together, and had bluntly informed them that it was her intention to again embark upon hazardous exploits.

When she had finished she offered to any, who did not care to follow her, a clearance with three months' pay. And it is indicative of the place she held in their affections when, from Captain Vaughan down, they one and all voted to remain.

Had she seen the men in their quarters afterwards, she would have a vivid impression of the effect her words had caused, full half-hour there was a riotous scene of enjoyment— a scene which not even the discipline-loving Hendricks attempted to quell.

For a few days the yacht had cruised about the Atlantic until Yvonne had formulated her plans for the immediate future. Before she had done so, however, she had spent many hours in the laboratory which ran clear across the after end of the Fleur-de-Lys.

What her experiments were not even Graves knew, but, had any been able to witness them, they could have seen that the principal object of her attention was a large, artificial bloom, daintily fashioned from purple silk. One thing, however, Graves did notice—that was the fact that her decision to return to England coincided with the completion of her experiments.

Orders were given to make for the English Channel, and at a quiet port on the Brittany coast of France the Fleur-de-Lys dropped anchor. Accompanied by Graves, Alec, and her maid Anna, Yvonne had entrained for Paris and thence to London, leaving the yacht anchored awaiting her orders.

Then had followed her application for and appointment to a place as typist with the Trott Manufacturing Co. of London—a place which she took under the name of "Miss Craig." How she had worked there for three weeks before she gained the information which was her object has already been seen, And now she was speeding along to her delightful place in Surrey, there to complete her arrangements for the coup she had planned.

Her decision to return to the place in Surrey had been wise in more ways than one. For three months it had been vacant, only her caretaker occupying the premises. Previous to that, during her long sojourn in London and her frequent periods of travel, it had been let to a Canadian family which had now returned to Canada.

Not since the early days of her adventurous career had she occupied it, and, thanks to Sexton Blake's discretion, it had never been recorded by Scotland Yard as a retreat of hers. Nor did any of the neighbouring inhabitants dream, for one moment, that the handsome, white-haired gentleman who, with his niece, sometimes occupied the fine old place was in the remotest degree connected with the famous Mademoiselle Yvonne. Care and foresight had guaranteed that.

Under Alec's hands the car made the old Tudor homestead under the two hours. Although the sky was clear and the sun blazed overhead there was a crisp autumn bite in the air, and Yvonne arrived both cold and hungry. She went at once to the library; where Graves sat before a big log fire reading.

"Hallo!" he said, smiling. "You came down quickly to-day. It seems no time since Alec left."

Yvonne nodded as she drew off her gloves.

"Yes. I didn't wait for anything. I suppose I should have lunched before leaving, but I have a lot to do and put it off."

"I'll ring and order something while you change."

"Thanks, uncle. Have it served in here, please. We can talk at the same time."

She departed to change while Graves rang and ordered a light lunch to be served in the library. It arrived simultaneously with Yvonne's reappearance, and while she picked daintily at it she informed Graves that she had left the Trott Manufacturing Co. for good.

"Why?" he asked. "Does that mean you intend moving?"

"Yes. I have succeeded in gaining the information I wanted."

"What do you intend doing, Yvonne?"

"It is better that you shouldn't know yet, uncle. I shall tell you after. Only what I propose doing will necessitate my going to London to-night,"

"Am I to go with you?"

"I think not. I shall motor through and take Alec. If all goes as I hope he can help me in all there is to do. But in order to carry out my plans I must make a move not later than tomorrow night. Since I am ready— or will be in a few hours—I have decided to go ahead to-night, I have planned carefully, and I don't anticipate any difficulty. And now I must go to the laboratory. I have a lot yet to do."

"Sure you'd rather go alone?" asked Graves.

For answer Yvonne bent swiftly and touched his forehead with her lips.

"Yes, please, uncle," she said softly. Then she was gone, and Graves turned back to his reading with a sigh.

On reaching the great room which she had turned into a laboratory Yvonne closed the door after her and turned the key. Once within its portals she seemed to become a different individual. All the girlish softness of manner seemed to disappear beneath the cold method of the scientist.

For scientist she was, and of a class far beyond the ordinary run. The elaborate fittings of the laboratory proved that it was no retreat of the dilettante, but the work-room of an enthusiast.

As far as had been possible, Yvonne had contrived to have it a copy of the laboratory on the Fleur-de-Lys. It was laid out with geometrical precision and, since the other had been copied in the arrangement, there was no delay in searching for articles needed.

The long, glass-topped experimenting-table was in the exact spot regarding the arrangement of the room as the one on the yacht. Likewise the crucibles, the small but powerful electric furnaces, the racks of test tubes, the shelves of chemicals and specimens, and even the scientific volumes which filled a case in one corner.

Her first proceeding was more of the nature of a locksmith's work than of the research scientist; but it was a necessary corollary to that which was to follow, and, with her usual care for details, Yvonne attended to it herself.

Drawing out the little leather bag from beneath the severely business-like blouse she had donned, she took out the piece of wax with which she had taken the impression of the keys in Morris's private office, and laid it on the experiment table.

Her next move was to make a mould of the two impressions. This took time and patience, but, when she had finished, she had two small articles which retained a perfect copy of the impressions in the wax. Laying these aside for the moment, she started one of the electric furnaces, and into a crucible placed a small lump of whitish metal.

Then she laid her watch on the experimenting-table, and, walking to the bookcase in the corner, drew out a volume entitled, "The Researches of Prof. Henry Boyle; A Treatise on the Properties of Coronium."[1]

With this in her hand, she seated herself before the glass-topped table, and immediately became immersed in the intricate and complex details of the researches of the above-named professor, only raising her head from time to time to turn a page or glance at her watch.

When exactly half an hour had passed, she closed the book with a snap and walked across to the crucible. Now the lump of white metal was a bubbling, silvery liquid, so, returning to the experimenting table, Yvonne picked up the two moulds she had made.

Tipping the crucible, with an unfaltering hand she filled first one then the other, laying them aside to cool. Then she turned off the electric heat and went back to the table.

"Before one can read one must open the book," she murmured. "Ergo, before I carry out my purpose, I must have keys. And now I have them."

Standing by the table, she cast her eyes over a row of vials set in racks overhead. One of these she lifted down, it contained a colourless liquid, which looked exactly like water or alcohol. But the care with which Yvonne handled it indicated that it was neither.

---

[1] a hypothetical chemical element thought to have been detected in the solar corona whose spectrum showed a number of lines later identified as belonging to iron, nickel, and other elements highly ionized at the extreme solar temperatures. See also Wiki   /drf

She set it on the table, and next took down a small wooden box. On being opened it revealed a muss of colour—heaps of purple and green. She carelessly upset it and, when the contents poured out on the table, it could be seen that they consisted of several artificial flowers.

The purple ones looked strangely similar to those made by the out-workers of the Trott Manufacturing Company. As a matter of fact they were, for Yvonne had procured them from Mrs. Harrison in Creig Street. The others, of a sickly green colour, had none of the richness or sheen of the purple blossoms. Yet in form they were exactly similar.

Yvonne left them on the table while she reached down a small spraying bulb from overhead. Then she removed the cork from the bottle of colourless liquid and, inserting the tip of the spray, let some of the liquid run up the tube.

Replacing the cork, she set the bottle aside gently, then picked up one of the purple flowers. Isolating it on the table, she laid down the spray and drew on a pair of rubber gloves.

Then she picked up the bulb and held it over the flower, gently pressing as she did so. A faint cloud of white vapour issued from the mouth of the bulb and settled upon the purple bloom. One pressure only she gave, then laid the spray aside.

For a few moments there was no perceptible change in the condition of the flower; but then, ever so slowly, the rich purple colour began to fade. Paler and paler it grew, until it was a pale violet, then a yellowish tinge appeared, then the same sickly, green colour of the flowers beside her.

At that it remained fixed, and when she held the changed bloom up to the light, it looked more like a tawdry bloom of cotton than the once rich purple it had been. Holding it thus, Yvonne began to speak as though addressing an invisible audience.

"Science can do much to-day," she said slowly. "It moves the wheels of commerce; it reads the riddle of the heavens; it enchains the dogs of war. Its discoveries, and the uses to which it puts them, are legion. It can imitate the most intricate processes of Nature's laboratory. And here is the proof.

"Who would think, in looking at those rich purple blooms, it they were made from anything less than the pure fibre of silkworm? In texture, in colour, in richness, they are perfect. Yet they are base. In endeavouring to change the colour from purple to something else, I discover what I suppose is one of the most closely-guarded secrets of the silk trade.

"When it was discovered not long ago that, by the crossing of wild Central American fibre blooms with the cotton plant, an excellent substitute for silk was formed, I must confess I thought little of it. But here before me is the proof that the substitute is as perfect as the genuine.

My liquid for eating away the purple colouring matter has accomplished two things. It has done as I intended; but it has also consumed the silken 'body' which the wild fibre plants have contributed, leaving the sheenless cotton in sickly solitude.

"Truly the Trott Manufacturing Company is due for a shock. Now to prepare a sufficient amount of the liquid, then I think I shall be ready. But there is one thing I must not forget. The watchman will have to be attended to."

Laying down the flower, Yvonne opened a drawer beneath the table and took out a spray, which was a larger edition of the one she had been using. She unscrewed the end of this one and cautiously emptied the contents of the bottle into it. Then she screwed on the cap and laid it aside.

Now she lifted down a huge bottle from an upper shelf, and from it refilled the smaller bottle. After replacing it, she crossed the laboratory, and from a case from the opposite wall took something which looked very much like a small automatic pistol. With this she returned to the experimenting table.

When she had snapped open the handle it could be seen that, instead of containing a place for cartridges, there was a small receptacle. Into this Yvonne poured some brownish liquid, and the initiated would have recognised the thing as a type of gas-gun—the extremely efficacious weapon which will render one unconscious for a length of time contingent upon the force of the charge used, but will not injure.

She laid the loaded weapon on the table and, opening another drawer beneath it, took out a small leather bag. Opening this, she gently placed inside the bottle of liquid, the large spray which she had filled, and the loaded gas-gun. That done, she closed the bag with a snap, and set it aside with extreme care.

Now she opened the moulds which had cooled, and there dropped on the table before her, two new, shiny keys. After a brief examination of these, she laid them beside the bag with a gesture of satisfaction, then gave a sigh.

"That is finished," she murmured, glancing at the clock.

"Already six. I have been longer than I thought. But I am ready. Now for an early dinner, then—London."

Unlocking the door, she turned off the light by which she had been working and left the laboratory, locking the door after her. She went direct to her room, where she dressed for dinner. She reached the wide hall at exactly seven, and heard Graves knocking the balls about in the billiard-room.

Passing through the small but beautifully arranged winter garden, she joined him. To her surprise he was already dressed.

"I was just coming to tell you it was time to dress, uncle," she smiled.

Graves waited until he had executed a neat cannon, then replied:

"I anticipated you, my dear. I had an idea you would dine early to-night. How did things go?"

"Splendidly. There wasn't a hitch. I repeated my experiments and found them quite as successful as before. By the way, uncle, do you know I have discovered something?"

"What is it?"

"Do you remember our discussion, some time ago, regarding the claim that a substitute for silk had been found by the crossing of wild Central American fibre blooms with the cotton plant?"

"Yes; it was one night in London, when Sexton Blake was there."

"Yes. If you remember he held that it was quite a reasonable theory. At the time I was very dubious. Well, I have discovered that it is so, and, moreover, I have found out that the product is being used commercially to-day.

"During one of my experiments, which was a colour experiment, I was startled to find that, when the chemical reaction had subsided, it had caused all the silk 'body' of the specimen to disappear, leaving behind nothing but cotton. I have repeated the experiment several times, and each time the result has been the same. It is marvellous what has been done by the cross-fertilisation of plants."

"Burbank started it," responded Graves, laying down his cue. "We have the seedless orange, the green and black carnation, and the spineless cactus, to mention only a few. Since it is probable that many plants were originally the outcome of accidental cross-fertilisation, it is only natural that carefully performed crossing should achieve much.

"Take wheat, for instance. By crossing and recrossing several different kinds, types of great value have been evolved —types which in rainless districts are great drought resisters, and give a yield which the ordinary type would not. But here comes the butler to announce dinner. Let us go in."

They made their way to the dining-room, still chatting over the subject of cross-fertilisation and, if the butler, who was serving the wine, listened at all, it must have been to wonder at his young mistress's remarkable grasp of a deep subject. Little did he dream that the whole discussion was the outcome of experiments leading to the confusion of one of the greatest London manufacturing companies.

After dinner, Yvonne went do her room and again changed. This time she donned a short golfing skirt, and on her feet put low shoes, having remarkable soles. They were straight and square and made of hard rubber—quite unlike any that usually protected her small feet.

Slipping into a jacket of the same material as the skirt, she then put on a close-fitting turban which came well down over the ears. About this, and concealing her features, she wound a thick motoring veil. That operation finished, she took from a drawer in the dressing-table a small automatic, which she examined and placed in the pocket of her jacket.

From her room she went to the laboratory where she first picked up the keys and thrust them in her pocket. Then she placed a pair of rubber gloves in the small instrument-bag which held the articles she had placed there earlier and, picking it up carefully, made her way out.

She went down a side staircase and out a small door, which opened on to a footpath leading to the garage. Along this she sped, until a light ahead revealed the shadowy outlines of a car, with a figure in the front seat.

"All ready, Alec," she said, climbing into the tonneau. "By the way, you did not forget to change your boots?"

"No, mademoiselle; I am all prepared."

"Then go ahead, Alec. It is just half-past eight. Don't drive too fast. If we reach London by eleven, it will be all right,"

With a nod Alec let in the clutch, and the car leaped forward down the elm-lined drive. All the way to London Yvonne lay back in a relaxed position. For the most of the way her eyes were closed. Only when they passed through a town or a village did she open them.

Her mind was on the business before her, and she was mentally considering every contingency in order to assure herself that she had guarded against every possible complication. The accomplishing of anything was to Yvonne like the picture to the artist or the story to the writer.

Not only must she create all the possible combinations which might arise, but she must be able to know beforehand what the effect of such combination must be, and how it would affect that which had already been done. Otherwise she was not satisfied, nor would she go ahead.

It is only the great who can see the fault of their own creations, and, at the same time, have the courage to destroy them. Yvonne was great in that way. Had she, at the last moment, discovered that she had neglected some minor detail which, though seemingly unimportant, might in the future give rise to some complication, she would not have gone ahead and risked it as would most. She would have had Alec turn back, and had it been impossible to arrange the detail by the time necessary, she would have abandoned her whole plan and patiently set about to devise another.

Perhaps it was this extraordinary capacity for thoroughness which in the past had made Yvonne not only a phenomenon in her adventurous career, but had lifted her to the front rank of present day scientists. And, by the same token, it was exactly the same quality which made Sexton Blake so extraordinarily successful in his profession.

But when they finally reached the suburbs of London, the car did not turn back. As far as she could think, Yvonne had done everything possible to assure the success of her plans.

Alec had his orders, and drove straight through the City by quiet streets until he reached the Bank. From there he picked a roundabout way until he was in the dark neighbourhood where the great building of the Trott Manufacturing Co. reared itself in gloomy silence.

Not a light could be seen, but Yvonne well knew that somewhere in the vast building was a watchman with his lantern. She realised that he was the most immediate danger, and to guard against that had been her reason for bringing the gas gun.

Alec drew up in the black shadows caused by a high building about fifty yards down from the factory. Then he shut off the engine and leaped out. Yvonne descended more leisurely, carrying the black instrument bag. Without a word, they moved along in the direction of the Trott Manufacturing Co.

Now, like a good many factories, the Trott building was built flush with the street, its many storeys stretching away to the rear out of view of people passing along. At first glance, one would scarcely think, high and impressive though it was, concealed such an expanse of walls and floors.

But Yvonne knew to a nicety what lay behind. Not for nothing had she spent a month there, seizing every opportunity to wander about. She had a perfect mental photograph of the interior of the place, and, once inside, would be able to move about with a minimum of uncertainty. Alec but followed her lead like a faithful dog.

Scarcely pausing to glance up and down the gloomy, narrow street, Yvonne entered the porch of the building, and drew out the larger key which she had cast that day. Inserting it in the keyhole, she turned. It worked as smoothly as one could wish, and the bolt shot back with only a faint click to indicate its movements. She turned the handle and entered, Alec close at her heels.

A wide flight of stairs stretched away from almost at their feet, and up they went, their rubber-soled shoes making no perceptible noise on the marble steps.

At the top there were two doors—one on the right, opening into the general office, and one on the left, opening into the executive offices of the firm. To the latter Yvonne turned. Now she brought the smaller key into use, and once again had the satisfaction of finding her castings had been perfect.

The door opened noiselessly, and they passed through. They were in a small waiting-room, off which opened several doors. The one on the extreme left Yvonne knew to be the board-room; that next to it, Sir Hector Trott's private room; the third, the secretary's office; the fourth, the office of Morris, manager; and the last, a door leading to the rear of the general offices, making it possible for communication to be held between them and the executive rooms without going by way of the landing.

She moved with certainty now. First she laid the small instrument bag on a nearby table, and, opening it, took out the gas gun. Then she closed the bag and handed it to Alec.

"Carry it very carefully, Alec. If you drop it, we are liable to be blown to bits."

Alec handled it with a care which showed he had no desire to end his existence per the medium of the roof, and followed Yvonne to the door connecting with the general office. Turning the handle, she entered a small passage, and waited for Alec.

"We must keep our eyes open, Alec. The night watchman may be prowling about in this part."

She moved on again, stepping with certainty. Every foot of the way was familiar to her, and when she reached the great room where the typists' desks were located, she passed between them without pausing.

She walked straight to door at the far end, and turned the handle gently. It opened at once, and Yvonne was about to step through, when, in the darkness ahead, she caught the gleam of a light. She made an imperative gesture for silence, and stood rigid, watching it.

When it still kept its position, it finally dawned upon her that either it was resting on the floor, or the night watchman, to whom it belonged, was standing perfectly still. Perhaps he heard them; and was listening in order to locate the sound.

Swaying backwards, Yvonne held her mouth close to Alec's ear.

"Stay here," she breathed, "I am going forward."

Without waiting for an answer, she dropped to her hands and knees, and began creeping along with the stealth of a panther. To right and left stretched long piles of cases—goods ready for shipment, she knew. Her way was along an alley formed by tiers, and at the far end was the light.

Foot by foot she went along, stopping every few moments to listen. Though she could see the light, she could not see the watchman. If he had grown suspicious, and were hiding in ambush, she would be in an awkward position. Then again he may have left the light there while he went to see after something in another room.

But a few moments later Yvonne grew rigid, as she saw a foot protruding from beyond the cases. The watchman was there! With infinite caution she proceeded still further until she could make out his trousered leg up to the knee. One hand was hanging loosely beside it.

Just then she heard a sound which, to her tautened nerves,

sounded like the crack of a gun. She jumped, then lay back, laughing silently. What she had heard had been a gentle snore. The watchman was asleep!

Swiftly she rose and took a few paces forward. It was only too true. He was seated upon an upturned case, his back resting against the last tier. On the floor at his feet was the lantern, while, beside it were the remains of his supper.

Yvonne contemplated him in silence for a moment, then she raised the gas gun, and, holding it close to his face, pulled the trigger. A cloud of vapour shot forth from the barrel, enveloping his face, and Yvonne leaped back to avoid the spreading fumes. The watchman's head drooped a little lower, and his body grew a trifle more relaxed. Those were the only signs he gave that the gun had done its work.

Now Yvonne sent a sibilant whisper along the alley between the cases, telling Alec to come on. He did so at once, and grinned appreciatively as he saw the watchman. From there Yvonne led the way along until they came to a steel door. This she opened and passed through. Then came a great room filled with machines, another door, another room, still another door, and finally they stepped into a room piled high with cases very similar to the first one.

"This is our destination, Alec. Do you see that white stretch over there?"

"Yes, mademoiselle."

"Those are cases, and I think the ones we are after. The fact that they are not piled one upon the other makes me think so. They appear to be still waiting for the covers to be nailed on. Besides, this is the room of which Johns is foreman. But come along. Get out your electric pocket torch, and we will soon see."

Alec passed her the bag and did as she bade. When the light from the torch lit up the scene, it was at once evident that Yvonne's deductions had been correct. Over at one side lay twenty large cases. Leaning against them were the covers, freshly stencilled, and the stencilled address was "Jarridge's," with underneath the figures "50 doz." Inside could be seen large cardboard boxes.

Yvonne nodded her head with satisfaction.

"That would just make it—fifty dozen to a case, and twenty cases in all. A thousand dozen was Jarridge's order. Open one of the cardboard boxes, Alec."

He lifted one out, and slipped off the cover. Before them lay a mass of purple blooms. Yvonne cast a quick glance at the cases.

"There must be five dozen in each cardboard box, Alec, for there are ten of the boxes in each case. At any rate, we shall soon know. Lift them out and lay them on the floor. Take the covers off, and as you finish each case go on to the next. I will follow you. We must work as quickly as possible. We don't want the car standing at the kerb too long."

With nimble fingers, Alec began taking the cardboard boxes out of the first case, laying them side by side on the floor with their covers off. Then he moved on to the second, and did the same there.

By now Yvonne had opened the black bag, and had taken out the loaded spray. Drawing on her rubber gloves, she bent over the cardboard boxes, and began spraying their contents. Box after box she sprayed, moving on to the next lot as Alec arranged them.

Once when she had sprayed the contents of about half the cases, she paused to refill the spray from the bottle she had brought along. Then she continued her work.

Alec had finished laying them out, and now moved back to the first case. Already the flowers there had changed to the sickly green colour which Yvonne had caused back in the laboratory. Rapidly he replaced the covers, and packed them back in the cases.

So quickly did he work, that, while Yvonne was still spraying the contents of the twentieth case, he was replacing the boxes of the nineteenth. Then he finished the last while Yvonne put back the spray and gloves in the bag. She cast a critical eye about when Alec had completed his task. Not a thing seemed different than when they had entered; not a trace of their work seemed to have been left behind.

With a nod of satisfaction, she picked up the bag and motioned to Alec to extinguish the torch. He thrust it in his pocket, and followed her back the way they had come. The night watchman still slumbered heavily on his box, and did not even stir as they passed him.

Then they were back in the general office, and passed on into the executive side. With the same infinite caution which had marked their entry, they made their departure, closing and locking the doors after them.

On reaching the street they stood in the shadow of the porch, listening, but no sound broke the stillness. It was well for the success of Yvonne's plans that the factory was situated in a quiet business street seldom favoured by the presence of a constable. As a matter of fact, not a single individual had passed along the street since they had arrived in the car.

They moved along to the car, keeping well in the shadow. Then, when Yvonne had entered the tonneau, Alec sent the car forward. A few moments later, and they were picking their way along through the night-bound streets of the City, heading for the open country.

From the time they had entered the factory until they had left had occupied just exactly forty-three minutes. Big Ben was just booming the hour of midnight as they passed along Whitehall and turned to pick up the Surrey road. Two hours later they flashed up the elm-lined drive of the old Tudor homestead, and entered the garage.

There was but one thing remaining to be done now and Yvonne did it without delay. Bidding Alec good-night, she entered the house by the way she had left it, and, creeping softly up the stairs, tiptoed along the silent halls to the laboratory. There she emptied the black bag of its contents, replacing the spray and gloves in their respective drawers, and the bottle, now scarcely half full of the colourless liquid, on the shelf above.

That done, she put the bag where it belonged, and turned to depart. As she paused to switch off the light, she murmured softly:

"That, I imagine, will cause you to think, Sir Hector Trott. And it is not the end of your lesson, either."

Then the light went out, and the strange, quixotic girl stole along to her room.

Yvonne proves an expert in the art of keymaking. *(See page 8.)*

The Second Chapter.   The Changed Blooms.

On the Holiday morning following Yvonne's midnight visit to the factory, Morris, the manager, entered his office with his usual brisk step, and seated himself before the heap of letters which awaited his attention. As he pressed a button for a stenographer, he remembered, with a frown, that the competent "Miss Craig" would not be there.

To the young lady who answered, he spoke curtly, and the fact that she had to ask him on several occasions to repeat did not tend to put him in a better humour. While she went out to type off the first batch, he rang for a boy, and ordered him to call Johns, the foreman.

When the latter appeared, the manager was still engrossed with his letters, but he looked up long enough to say:

"I sent for you, Johns, to ask about the Jarridge order. It went all right, I presume?"

"Yes, sir. The cases were nailed up the first thing, and left here on the motor lorry at eight o'clock. They will have them already."

"Very well, Johns; that is all. There is an order here from South Africa. It will need special attention, but I haven't time now to discuss it. I will send for you later on."

The foreman withdrew, and the manager turned back to his letters. He had read less than half a page of the one he held in his hand when his desk telephone buzzed noisily. Picking up the receiver, he said curtly:

"Hallo!"

The voice of the telephone operator in the outer office answered him.

"Jarridge's are calling, Mr. Morris. I'll switch them on.

He waited for a moment, then there was a click, and over the line came a masculine voice.

"Hallo, hallo!"

"Hallo!" called back Morris. "This is the Trott Manufacturing Company."

"Oh, is that Mr. Morris, the manager, speaking?"

"Yes. Who is it?"

"This is Colwell, of Jarridge's."

"Yes, Mr. Colwell," said Morris suavely. "What is it?"

"I called up to tell you that you have made a mistake in the delivery of that flower order," replied Colwell.

"Impossible!" blurted Morris. "What do you mean?"

"Do you remember our order?" came back Colwell's voice frigidly.

"Perfectly. It was for one thousand dozen artificial blooms of purple silk."

"That was my impression also. Therefore, will you kindly tell me why you have sent us one thousand dozen blooms of the most hideous green imaginable, and of cotton at that?"

"One thousand blooms of green, and— Oh, you must be joking, Mr. Colwell."

"I assure you I was never more serious in my life."

"Have you opened all the cases? Perhaps a box of wrong kind got mixed in by mistake."

"I thought that might be the case, so had them all opened. They are the same throughout—green chiton flowers."

"Were the cases addressed to you?"

"They are stencilled 'Jarridge's.'"

"Then there has been some mistake, Mr. Colwell. The packers have stencilled the wrong cases, although I did not know we had any green cotton blooms in stock. I shall interview the foreman at once, and have the mistake rectified. I will also have the purple blooms sent on immediately, and the team can bring back the others. I am very, very sorry that the mistake occurred."

"It wouldn't matter so much, only one of our big sale begins this morning, and we have made a special feature of the artificial blooms. The crowds will be here any time now, so please rush them."

"I shall start them off at once."

When Morris rang off, he leaned forward with a heavy frown, and pressed a button. To the boy who answered the ring, he snapped:

"Tell Johns, the foreman, to come here at once."

The boy sped away on his errand, and while he waited, the manager tapped the desk irritably. Johns appeared breathing heavily. The boy's message had brought him on the run.

"What kind of idiots have you in your department, Johns?" stormed the manager. "Here we make a special effort to get a slice of Jarridge's business, and the very first is bungled. How did it happen that the wrong cases were stencilled and sent?"

"The wrong cases stencilled and sent!" echoed the foreman, with a look of blank amazement on his face. "I don't understand you, sir."

Morris made a visible effort to contain himself.

"Look here, Johns," he said, with dangerous calm. "What was the order for Jarridge's?"

"One thousand dozen purple silk blooms," answered the foreman promptly.

"Exactly. The blooms I inspected myself, on Saturday morning was the order, was it not?"

"Certainly, sir. We had no other blooms in stock."

"Then how do you explain the fact that Jarridge's were sent one thousand dozen green cotton blooms by mistake? And another thing, who ordered those last? I knew nothing about them. If I find out who is responsible for this mistake, there is going to be trouble for him.

"Jarridge's are wild, and I don't blame them. There is only one thing to be done how, and that is to send the purple blooms at once. Get one of the motor lorries, and hustle them along. Have those other blooms brought back, and let me know when they arrive. I'll find out who has been putting green cotton blooms in stock without my authority."

The foreman's throat was working like that of a man in the throes of apoplexy. He was gazing at his superior as though the latter had suddenly taken leave of his senses. Finally, he managed to articulate:

"I—I beg your pardon, Mr. Morris, but I don't think I heard you aright. Green chiton blooms! We never had any in stock, sir. And the Jarridge order left here perfectly correct in every detail.

"The cases were on the floor by the shipping door, waiting for the covers. I superintended the nailing of them myself, and saw them loaded. There has been no other order of that kind sent from here this morning."

The manager glared at the foreman for a moment, then his wrath broke all bounds.

"What do you mean?" he cried, in a torrent of rage. "Are you mad? I tell you the wrong order was sent to Jarridge's. They have just called up and said so. One thousand dozen green cotton blooms were sent them by mistake."

At this point the foreman interrupted.

"Mr. Morris," he said quietly, "if the wrong order was sent to Jarridge's, and since no other order of that nature has been sent out this morning, then the purple blooms should still be here, shouldn't they?"

The manager calmed down as he realised the force of the other's logic. Jumping to his feet, he started for the door.

"Come along! We will investigate this muddle."

The foreman followed him along through the various rooms where the operatives worked busily, until he reached the room over which Johns was foreman. Several men were working on tiers of cases, but to these Morris paid no heed. He made straight for the vacant space by the shipping door.

Now there were no signs of the cases which had littered the space on Saturday. Standing by the door the manager pointed.

"On Saturday morning I inspected the purple blooms. They were packed in twenty cases, which lay on the floor just here."

"Yes, sir."

"What has become of those cases?"

"They have been sent to Jarridge's, sir."

"You still insist on that, Johns?"

"Yes, sir. Those cases were here when I came this morning. I had them nailed on and sent them at once."

"Did you examine the contents?"

"No, sir. But it wasn't necessary. You said Saturday that they were perfectly satisfactory."

"And you still claim that no mistake could have been made?"

"It could not, Mr. Morris. Listen, sir! I was the last to this room on Saturday. When I left the cases were still before the door. I was the first here this morning. The cases here just as they had been on Saturday.

"None of the men had been working about, and, besides, they would not take it upon themselves to shift twenty big cases without my order. If we had had a second lot of twenty cases to go out they should have been piled further back.

"It was quite understood that the Jarridge order should be the first to go. More than that, Mr. Morris, the Jarridge order was the only order on the floor for shipment. Therefore, a mistake was impossible.

"I think you said something about green cotton blooms, sir. Well, if Jarridge's received a lot of green blooms, they never received them from us. The purple silk blooms which were sent were the only artificial flowers in this department. I know that for a fact. To my knowledge we have never had any green cotton blooms in stock, and that covers fourteen years."

At that moment Morris was easily the angriest and most puzzled man in the City of London. He felt that either Colwell of Jarridge's, the foreman, or himself had suddenly gone mad; but for the moment he didn't decide which one. He was beginning to realise that the situation was one demanding cool handling, and that nothing was to be gained by a show of temper. When Johns had quite finished, he looked about.

"Then am I to understand, Johns, that, whether or not a mistake has been made, you have no purple blooms in stock?"

"Not one, sir. I'll stake my life there isn't a purple bloom in the place. Why, sir, they were coming in from the outworkers up to closing time on Saturday."

"Then if a mistake of some kind had been made, we could not send any to Jarridge's?"

"They have already been sent to them, sir," responded Johns doggedly.

The manager turned.

"Get on your hat and coat, Johns. We will go along to Jarridge's and investigate things there."

The foreman obeyed at once, and followed the manager to his private office. There Morris got his own hat, and they passed out to the street. Hailing a taxi, the manager climbed in, and motioned Johns to do likewise. A quarter of an hour later they were being ushered into the office of Colwell, the assistant manager of Jarridge's.

Morris wasted no time in coming to the point.

"Mr. Colwell," he said, "are you quite certain that the green blooms you unpacked were the cases from our factory? Would it be possible that your men had confused our order with one from another factory?"

Colwell glanced up in surprise.

"Quite impossible, Mr. Morris," he said briefly. "Your order was the only one we had of that description. But why do you ask?"

"Because my foreman here insists that there was no mistake in the goods sent to you."

"Perhaps you would like to see the cases for yourself, Mr. Morris?"

"That is what I was going to suggest."

"Then come with me, please."

Colwell rose and the other two followed him through several great retail departments until they came to a large goods receiving room. Here Colwell motioned to a man who stood at a desk checking invoices.

"Potterson, where are those cases which arrived from the Trott Manufacturing Co.?"

"Over there, sir. Do you wish to see them?"

"Yes."

The whole party moved along past a littered array of cases and boxes until they came to twenty large cases standing by themselves. Both Morris and Johns hastened forward at once and bent over them.

"They are our cases all right, sir," said the foreman.

But Morris was busy extracting one of the cardboard boxes from a case near at hand. As he prised off the cover he gave an exclamation of utter amazement which brought the others crowding about him. Instead of the rich purple blooms with which the box should have been filled; he was gazing upon a mass of tawdry cotton flowers of the most hideous green shade.

Dropping the box he snatched up another and another. Every one was the same— sickly green instead of blazing purple. He tossed the last one aside with a gesture of despair. Then he turned to the foreman.

"Well, Johns, what have you to say?"

The foreman was examining one of the cardboard boxes.

These cases came from our factory, Mr. Morris, and these boxes are the same which we use. They bear the same number on the bottom. But those flowers never came from the Trott Manufacturing Co. I'll stake my life on that."

At that moment, Colwell's voice broke in.

"What do you mean by that remark?" he asked coldly. "Are you intimating that these boxes were packed by Jarridge's?"

"No, sir, I am not. But at the same time they never came from our place. Saturday morning these very boxes were full of purple flowers, I'll swear to that.

"Mr. Morris inspected them and passed them. They were not touched until the covers were nailed on. Then they were sent on here. Besides, no such flowers as these green blooms were ever in stock at the Trott Manufacturing Co. We never handle goods of that quality.

"Johns is perfectly right about that," put in Morris. "I can also vouch that the boxes were full of the proper flowers on Saturday."

Colwell turned to his checking clerk.

"Potterson, who received these goods?"

"I did, sir."

"Are they exactly as you received them?"

"Yes, sir, exactly."

"How did they arrive?"

"By a motor lorry, bearing the name of the Trott Manufacturing Co. I signed for them in the ordinary way."

"How long was it after you opened the cases that you sent for me?"

"At once, sir. I knew they should have been purple."

Then Colwell turned to Morris.

"When Potterson sent for me, Mr. Morris, I came down at once. Then I 'phoned you. I can assure you that these goods are exactly as they arrived from your factory. A mistake has been made, but it hasn't occurred at this end.

"We gave you an order for one thousand dozen purple silk blooms. We have your letter guaranteeing their delivery for this morning. On the basis of that we advertised them in our sale.

"I am sorry that there is a mistake on your part, but, at the same time, I must insist on the immediate delivery of the order. The people are already asking where they are. If they do not arrive inside an hour I shall have to cancel the order and demand damages.

"Needless to say, Mr. Morris, this occurrence has not increased our desire to do business with the Trott Manufacturing Co. I shall wait one hour for the goods. After that, if they have not arrived you may consider the account closed. Also I shall be obliged if you will have this green nightmare removed. And now I must ask you to excuse me as I am very busy."

Morris made no reply. What had he to say? Nothing. It was hard to stand there and listen to Colwell's remarks, but argument would only have aggravated matters. So he turned and with Johns in his wake sought the street. Not a word did he speak the whole way back to the factory.

On arriving there he at once went to the shipping room. There he called for the shipping book and examined the record of every order, large or small, which had left the factory that day. When he had a full list he sent for the chief clerk and ordered him to have a thorough examination made at once in order to discover if any of the goods sent out had contained amongst them any purple blooms.

That done he stood by while the shipping-room employees opened and exhibited to his view the contents of every case in the place. So thorough was the inspection that it was past noon when they finished. But not the faintest sign of a purple bloom did they find.

Just as the last case was replaced the lorry returned with the twenty cases from Jarridge's, and simultaneous with their arrival appeared the chief clerk. He reported that full inquiries had been made, but that there had been no irregularity in any of the orders sent out. None of them had contained any purple flowers.

Morris nodded curtly as he received the report; then directed that the twenty returned cases should be piled to one side. Then he called the foreman.

"Johns, have you any silk left such as you supplied to the out-workers for those purple blooms.

"Yes, sir. We have several bolts still on hand."

"Get me about a yard of it, and also a piece of the wire used. Bring them to my office with a box of those green flowers. Then get ahead with the day's work."

"About Jarridge's, sir?" asked the foreman tentatively.

"There is only one thing to be done," snapped the manager. "I shall have to telephone them that the goods cannot be delivered. A pretty mess altogether. But I tell you straight, Johns, that I am going to stick on this until I find out who is the guilty party.

"As near as I can figure out one thousand dozen purple blooms have completely disappeared. They were worth at cost price for labour, silk and wire, over a thousand pounds. In addition to that we have lost the profit on the sale which would have meant another thousand. And, from nowhere, there suddenly appears a trashy mess of flowers not worth a shilling a dozen.

"It is a case for the police, and unless I am very much mistaken, they will be on the matter before the day is over. So if there is anyone in the place who knows anything about it, now is the time for him to speak up."

With that Morris stamped away, leaving Johns, the foreman, in a very uncomfortable frame of mind.

⋅　　⋅　　⋅　　⋅　　⋅

So beautifully oiled was the executive machinery of the Trott

Manufacturing Co. that it was rare indeed for Sir Hector Trott, the supreme head of the organisation, to be called in for consultation. Ordinarily he was left to pursue his golfing, and yachting, and racing undisturbed, while the cogs of his business ran smoothly along.

To do him credit it was his own magnificent genius for organisation which had made this possible, and, since he was but tasting the fruits of his own efforts none could begrudge them to him. In the early days, before he had risen to the pinnacle he now occupied, he had worked early and late, and certainly he could thank none but himself and his own energy for the position he had attained.

That a large portion of his profits were gained by systems of sweating, did not militate against him in the eyes of his fellows. He but did as other factories which employed outworkers did, and, if he at times felt slight twinges of his conscience, he dulled them by another contribution to one of his pet charities.

He closed his eyes to the abuse which was going on, and reckoned his magnificent gifts more than balanced his account with the sweated beings. That is where Yvonne disagreed with his theory of life, and is why she had chosen him to be the recipient of a drastic lesson.

Who was in the right and who in the wrong belongs to a comprehensive treatise on sociology. Certainly Sir Hector Trott's greatest wrong was to be a party to the iniquitous system of sweating. Yvonne's greatest motive was a desire to alleviate some of the suffering caused by the system, and to bring home to those who were responsible for it a full realisation of its meaning to the victims.

But on this Monday morning Sir Hector was to be compelled to forgo the motoring trip he had promised himself, for, on reaching his private office, Morris, the manager, called him up at once asking him to come to the factory on urgent business. Half an hour afterwards, Sir Hector arrived and hustled in.

He was a robust-looking man in the later fifties, with a florid countenance and close-cropped side whiskers. The rest of his face was clean shaven, and showed the remains of once firm features, whose outline was now spoiled by an overplus of flesh. In other words, Sir Hector was stout. He carried himself alertly however, and when he spoke his voice was coldly businesslike.

"What is it, Morris?" he asked as he seated himself. "Nothing wrong, I hope?"

"I am sorry, Sir Hector; but there is a great deal wrong. Will you listen, please, and I will tell you the whole facts?"

The baronet nodded for him to proceed. Forthwith Morris began. He told of his persistent efforts to get a share of Jarridge's business, and how, at last, he had secured an initial order for one thousand dozen purple blooms.

He went on to describe how it had been necessary to rush the order, and how on Saturday he had inspected it, finding everything satisfactory. Then he related what had occurred since his arrival at the office that morning, including the exhaustive but fruitless investigations he had made.

Throughout the whole recital, Sir Hector sat leaning back with closed eyes. The casual onlooker might have thought he displayed little interest in the manager's tale, but the latter knew his chief well. He knew that the keen mind which had built up the Trott Manufacturing Co. was grasping every detail of the story, analysing it thoroughly and anticipating much that was to follow.

When Morris had finished, the baronet sat up.

"Let me see the silk, wire and green flowers, Morris."

The manager handed over the articles he had received from the foreman, and watched Sir Hector while he examined them. In a few moments he passed them back.

"'You said the cases and cardboard boxes containing the green flowers which you sent to Jarridge's were the same as we used?"

"Yes, sir. The cases were ours and the boxes exactly similar to others which we have in stock. They bore the same series number on the bottom."

"Well, the wire in this green flower is the same which was used for the purple flowers, Morris, if this piece I hold here is a sample."

"It is, sir."

"It is exactly similar. You can see for yourself. It is no case of thieving, Morris. It is bigger than that."

"What do you make of it, sir?"

"Plot, Morris, plot."

"I don't quite follow, Sir Hector."

"My dear fellow, it is impossible for me to read its meaning, but of this I am certain. We have been the victim of a plot. The chances are it is the work of someone interested in seeing our business relations with Jarridge's broken off.

"It is difficult to imagine how the thing was done, but there is the visible proof. It is very probable that the plotters have an accomplice here in the factory. We are only on really unfriendly terms with one of our competitors—the Swift Silk Co, But I do not think they would stoop to such methods as these.

"At the same time, Morris, you must ferret out the truth. It is no case for you—the business requires every moment of your attention. Nor is it a case for the police. They would still be bungling over it in a month's time. It is a case for quick action and quick results, and there is only one man I know of from whom we can expect those."

"Who is that, sir?"

"Sexton Blake. Send for him at once, Morris."

Without giving the manager time to reply the baronet was on his feet, making for the door. There he paused for a moment.

"Let me know if you find anything important, Morris. Otherwise don't bother me with it."

Then he was gone, leaving the manager to wrestle with the difficulty in his own way. But Morris realised fully the sound truth of Sir Hector's words, and scarcely had his chief disappeared than he lifted the telephone receiver.

Telling the operator in the outer office to get Sexton Blake on the 'phone he leaned back and waited. In a few minutes the instrument on his desk rang, and he again picked up the receiver.

"Hallo! Hallo!" he said. "Is this Mr. Sexton Blake speaking?"

"It is," came back in incisive tones. "Who are you?"

"This is the manager of the Trott Manufacturing Co. speaking, Mr. Blake. Are you engaged this morning?"

"It all depends," replied the cold tones. "What is wrong?"

"A matter of some importance, Mr. Blake. If you could make it convenient to call here, I should be greatly obliged. I can't say more over the 'phone."

"I shall be there in thirty minutes," answered Blake, and Morris heard the 'phone click as the receiver was hung up.

As he replaced his own he lighted a cigar and murmured:

"Now, we'll see what we can make of this affair, Mr. Sexton Blake. If you can tell me what has become of those purple blooms, and from whence those green nightmares came, I shall believe some of the wonderful reports I have heard of you. At any rate, Sir Hector did not seem to doubt your ability. I only hope you can justify his confidence in it."

Then the manager fell to musing, and not until an office boy entered thirty minutes later to announce a visitor did he move. He swung round and saw a tall, well-built man coming towards him. His gaze took in the alert carriage of the body, the high white forehead and stern features, backed up by the steely grey eyes, and he knew that before him stood the man of whom he had heard so much—Sexton Blake.

IN listening to the story of the manager Blake showed a strange similarity of attitude to that adopted by Sir Hector Trott under the same circumstances. His greeting had been of the briefest, and with his usual brusqueness he had asked the other to come to the point.

In substance the story was the same as that told to the baronet. Realising that he was speaking to a famous detective, Morris dwelt at greater length on the thoroughness of his own investigations, but the facts were essentially the same.

When he had quite finished he leaned back with an air which seemed to say: "There you are, Mister Man. I guess you will find that a hard nut to crack." It was entirely wasted, however, for Blake did not see it. He was deep in thought.

Not a syllable of the story had he missed; not a possible suggestion of any one point had escaped him. Already was he arranging the skeleton upon which to reconstruct the affair. Even now was the great sweep of the mental circle being drawn within which he would array all the items. But he confessed to himself that the present circle must indeed be large in order to accommodate the multitudinous facts, if not a greatness of time.

As he tentatively outlined it, the case stood thus: Between one o'clock on Saturday and early Monday morning one thousand dozen purple silk blooms had mysteriously disappeared, from the warehouse of the Trott Manufacturing Co., and in their place had appeared an equal number of shoddy green, cotton blooms. That was the meat of the affair. It was the basic mystery which he must unravel. All other facts and suggestions but led up to or away from the central point.

In a way, the case contained an exceptional number of incidents—a circumstance which naturally rendered solution more difficult. The circle must include not only the employees of the factory, but it must encompass the receiving room at Jarridge's and the time spent in the delivery of the cases.

But with nothing but the bare facts to go on analyses and deductions were premature. Questions which would never occur to the layman must be asked in order to elicit further information, and these might arouse a host of suggestions in the trained mind of the investigator. But though Morris was prepared to be cross-examined he certainly did not expect the question which Blake put first.

"What time do you close on Saturdays, Mr. Morris?"

"At one o clock," replied the latter in surprise.

"Does everybody leave at that hour?"

"Yes!"

"There was no change in the ordinary course last Saturday? No one stayed for overtime?"

"No, we closed sharp at one. I myself came back at three to sign some letters. I was here until five."

"There is a watchman, of course?"

"Yes. During the week-end a man goes on duty at two o'clock on Saturday afternoon. He stays on until ten at night. Then the regular watchman goes on until six Sunday morning. He is then relieved by the other who is on during the day. Then the regular man goes on until Monday morning.

"I see. I shall wish to interview them both. Do they live near here?"

"In the next street. Do you wish to see them at once?"

"Please."

Morris turned and pressed a button in his desk. A boy answered almost immediately.

"Find Jacobs and Thomas, the two watchmen," he ordered. "Tell them I want to see them here as soon as they can come."

As the boy sped away Blake proceeded with his questioning. "Have you interviewed either of them yet?"

"No! It never occurred to me. And I can't see your object either, Mr. Blake. Do you think someone entered the factory during the week-end?"

"The blossoms did not change of their own accord," commented Blake drily, "While we are waiting for the watchmen I should like to examine the shipping-room."

Morris rose at once.

"Don't you wish to examine the silk and other articles—wire and green bloom?"

"Not yet, thanks, Afterwards I shall have a look at them."

They went along to the shipping-room where Blake sauntered about apparently very interested. Yet during the fifteen minutes he was there his eagle eyes had taken in not only the whole plan of the place, including the arrangement of windows and doors but had studied the features of every employee.

When they returned to the manager's office they found the two watchmen had arrived. Blake had them in separately. The first to enter was Jacobs. He had been on day duty and answered Blake's questions readily.

"Your name is?"

"Jacobs, sir."

"You were on duty here on Saturday?"

"Yes, sir. From two o'clock in the afternoon until ten at night."

"Who relieved you?"

"Thomas, the other watchman."

"You returned to duty when?"

"Sunday morning, sir. I went off at nine, Sunday night."

"And Thomas relieved you again?

"Yes, sir."

"You made your rounds regularly?"

"Yes, sir."

"Did you, either on Saturday or Sunday, see anything out of the ordinary? Think carefully, now. Try and remember if there was the slightest thing which struck you."

The man knit his brows.

"I can't think of anything, sir."

"You were in the shipping-room over which Johns is foreman?"

"Yes, sir."

"How often?"

"Two or three times each day."

"Do you remember seeing some open cases near the door, ready for shipment?"

"Oh, yes, sir."

"And no time noticed any change in their arrangement?"

"No, sir."

"What time was it when you were last there?"

"About six o'clock Sunday evening, sir."

"Very well, Jacobs, that will do. Send in Thomas when you go out."

The man retired and a moment later Thomas appeared. He stood nervously waiting.

"Thomas," said Blake curtly, "you went on duty at ten o'clock Saturday night, did you not?"

"Yes, sir."

"And were on until Sunday morning?"

"Yes, sir."

"You went on again on Sunday night?"

"Yes, sir."

"Now, think carefully. During Saturday night or Sunday night, did anything out of the ordinary occur?"

"No, sir."

"Absolutely nothing! Be perfectly sure, Thomas. It is important that we should know. You saw nothing—heard nothing—remember nothing?"

"No, sir."

"You went about your duties as usual?"

"Yes, sir."

"Let us take Saturday night first, Thomas. You made your rounds, how often?"

"Twice, sir."

"Why only twice?" broke in the manager sharply, "Three times is the number you are supposed to make."

Blake raised his hand.

"One moment, Mr. Morris. I am conducting this affair. Please do not interfere."

Then he turned to the watchman.

"You said you made your rounds twice on Saturday night?"

"Yes, sir."

"At what time?"

"I made the first one at half-past ten, sir, and the second at four."

"Rather a long time in between, wasn't it, Thomas?"

"Yes, sir," answered the man with a touch of sullenness.

"Now let us take Sunday night, Thomas," went on Blake imperturbably. "How often did you make your rounds Sunday night?"

"Three times."

"Ah! Why three times on Sunday night, Thomas, and only twice on Saturday night?"

The man was silent.

"I am waiting, Thomas," said Blake quietly.

Still the other preserved a dogged silence.

"Shall I tell you why?" asked Blake pleasantly.

Thomas glanced at him swiftly.

"Wasn't it because you were taking a nap?" suggested Blake,

with a sudden snap in his voice.

The man nodded.

"Yes," he confessed.

"I thought so. When a night watchman cannot account for something like five hours it is usually because he has been asleep, Thomas. Now supposing you be a little more frank? Tell me about it."

"I can't imagine how it happened," replied the man, in a low tone, "I had my supper after making my first round. When I had finished I felt drowsy. I leaned back and dozed. I often do, and it has never lasted more than five minutes. That is all I remember.

"When I woke up I thought I had been asleep about ten minutes, I started at once to make a round of the offices, and when I got there saw it was four o'clock. It gave me a turn. I was worried, and made a round of the whole factory at once."

"And everything was all right?"

"Exactly as usual."

"You visited the room over which Johns is foreman?"

"Yes, sir."

"Do you remember the cases near the door waiting to be shipped?"

"Yes, sir."

"They were quite as usual?"

"Yes, sir."

"And also on Sunday night?"

"Yes, sir."

"Very well, Thomas; you may go now."

The man backed out as though glad to escape. As the door closed upon him Blake turned to the manager.

"If you will give me the piece of purple silk which you spoke of, as well as a length of the wire and a few of those green blooms, I shall take them along with me, Mr. Morris," he said.

"You don't wish to see anything further here?" asked the other, in surprise.

"Not at present. I want to ask you just one or two more questions; then I shall go. How long is it since you received Jarridge's order for the blooms?"

"Six weeks."

"Is there any correspondence on the matter?"

"I have one or two letters. Do you wish to see them?"

"Please"

Morris rose and took down a letter-file bearing the initial "J." Opening it, he drew out two sheets of paper.

"There are just two," he said, passing them over. "The first is, as you see, a confirmation of the order, and dated about six weeks ago. The other is an inquiry as to when the goods would be delivered."

Blake was reading the latter.

"I see this is dated about ten days ago," he said, tapping it with his finger.

"Yes."

"You replied to it by letter or 'phone?"

"By letter."

"Have you a copy?"

"Yes. One moment, and I will get it."

From a stand he brought another file labelled "Orders J." Opening it, he drew out two more sheets of paper.

"One of those is a copy of the order; the other is my reply to the inquiry."

Blake merely glanced at the order, then studied the letter.

"This is a carbon copy, I see."

"Yes,"

"It is initialed here 'F. L. M.—M. C.' I presume 'F. L. M.' means, you?"

"Yes. Those initials indicate by whom the letter was dictated, and which typist took it."

"I see. Then 'M. C.' is the typist?"

"Yes."

"Is she in at present?"

Morris knit his brows.

"M. C. Let me think. That would be—why, yes, that is Miss Craig! No, she is not here. She has left."

"Ah! Recently?"

"She left on Saturday last."

"Did she give notice?"

"Yes. Now I think of it, she gave notice while I was dictating to her on Monday."

"Had you dictated this letter?"

"I am not sure, but I think so."

"Try to remember."

"I think—yes, I am quite positive I had. But why do you ask, Mr. Blake? Miss Craig could have had nothing to do with this."

"I didn't suggest that she had," replied Blake. "I am merely trying to get a line on everything which touches the case. How long was she with you?"

"About a month."

"What did she look like?"

"Ask me something easy. She was a girl who struck me as being better looking than the average. And she was the best typist I ever had. I was sorry to lose her."

"Describe her, man. I can tell nothing from that."

"Well, she always dressed in blue, for one thing. She was medium height, rather slim, and had red hair."

Blake smiled.

"I am afraid you would never make a detective, Mr. Morris. What was her reason for leaving? Any trouble?"

"No. She said her own affairs made it essential."

"Have you her address?"

"They will have it in the office; I will ring and get it."

He pressed a button, and while waiting for the boy scribbled a note to the cashier asking for Miss Craig's address. In ten minutes the boy brought back a slip of paper, which the manager handed to Blake. The latter stuffed it in his pocket without looking at it. Then he again rose.

"I shall go along now, Mr. Morris, and investigate one or two points which have occurred to me. I may need to see you again, and if I do will call you up."

"All right Mr. Blake. I'd like to say that I am keen to have this affair straightened out. Sir Hector looks to me, I know."

"I shall do my best." responded Blake non-committally.

With that, he shook hands and left, taking with him the piece of purple silk, the length of wire and several of the tawdry green blooms. At the kerb outside his car was waiting with Tinker at the wheel.

"Home, my lad," said Blake, stepping in.

As Tinker started off he turned his head, "Anything doing, guv'nor?"

"I think so, Tinker. Rather a curious case. It presents one or two features which are quite extraordinary, I shall tell you about it when we reach home."

On arriving at Baker Street, they went in at once, and seating himself at the desk Blake gave Tinker an outline of the case.

"You can see my lad what features I referred to as being peculiar," he said, when he had finished. "Now I want you to go to this address in Bloomsbury. Doubtless it is a boarding establishment. Find out if Miss Craig is known there. If she is, inquire if she is staying there at present, or if not, when she left. Then drive straight back here. In the meantime I shall follow up one or two other lines."

Tinker hurried out, bearing the slip of paper which Blake handed him, and a moment later Blake heard the car as it moved on. He himself rose, and, gathering up the articles Morris had given him, made his way to the laboratory. He laid them on the experimenting table until he had donned his white jacket; then bent over them.

He first gave his attention to the length of fine wire. He examined it with the naked eye and through a magnifying glass. He bent it and twisted it and straightened it. Then he laid it aside.

Next he picked up one of the green cotton blooms. With careful fingers he untwisted the wire which held it in shape, and removed the cloth from it. This he spread out on the experimenting table, and left it there until he had adjusted his microscope.

After that he fixed a piece of the cotton on a slab, and applied his eye to the eyepiece. The seemingly smooth cloth now appeared like a vast desert crossed and recrossed by giant gullies and streams. After studying it for the space of five minutes, Blake lifted his head and removed the slide.

Next he cut off a small piece of the purple silk and placed it on the slide. Once more he applied his eye to the instrument, and gazed at the purple landscape stretched before him. At first it seemed totally different to the green desert upon which he had gazed. It was deep and rich in colouring, reminding one of deep purple forests. Over it all was a glittering sheen like a great stretch of shimmering dew.

But as the minutes passed Blake's eyes pierced the purple forests, and beneath them he made out a criss-cross arrangement of gullies strangely like those on the green desert.

He raised his head swiftly, and, taking the purple piece from the slide, again put on the bit of green cotton. This time he studied it with even greater care, but when he finally lifted his head there was a glitter of interest in his eyes.

"Impossible!"

Whatever he may have considered as being impossible did not deter him from reaching to a shelf above and taking down a large bottle of colourless liquid which was labelled with cryptic letters. Next he reached for a spray, and, taking the glass stopper from the bottle, filled the bulb.

Then he replaced the stopper, and bent over the bit of purple silk. With a steady hand he sprayed it thoroughly; then he waited. A minute—two minutes—three minutes passed. The bit of silk exhibited not the slightest change.

With a shrug, Blake emptied the remaining contents of the spray back in the bottle, and replaced it on the shelf. Now he took down another bottle containing a cloudy mixture which, on being opened, smelled not unlike ammonia. He drew a little of this into the spray, and cutting off another small bit of silk, pressed the bulb. Disappointment again! The only change was to cause the rich purple to turn blackish.

Bottle after bottle he tried on bits of the silk. Now it was a colour test, now a texture test, now an acid test. One and all were disappointing. At last he raised his head, with a puzzled look.

"I didn't expect it, but, at the same time, the coincidence of those lines is queer. Let me see now! By thunder. I wonder—I wonder."

As a thought came to him he sprang forward and reached down a small bottle which was filled with a colourless liquid not unlike that in the first bottle. For this test he got a fresh spray, and removing the stopper of the bottle, carefully drew out a little of the liquid. Then he replaced the stopper, and cautiously set the bottle back in its place.

"Dangerous stuff," he muttered "Must handle it gently."

He now cut off another small piece of the purple silk, and placing it on a glass slide, picked up the spray. He saturated the silk thoroughly with the white vapour which came forth, and then laid the spray aside.

Almost at once a change was visible. The rich purple began to fade to violet. Paler still it grew, until it was of a yellowish shade; then suddenly it changed to green—the same sickly green of the blooms he had brought with him from the factory.

Blake watched in utter amazement. He had taken a long chance— a chance which he had little expected to produce results. That the change which he had just seen was to occur he had not expected. It was merely the result of his usual persistency and his desire not to let any chance go untried. And here, to his utter surprise, he had "struck gold."

With, swiftly-working fingers he placed the bit of green on the slide and pushed it into the microscope. One long look he took at it, then he straightened himself and began pacing up and down,

"It is almost unbelievable," he muttered, chewing at an unlit cigar. "It was but a hazard, and it proved itself. But, who could have dreamed it—for it is so? That piece of rich purple silk is not true silk as produced by the silkworm. Nor is it artificial silk as produced in commercial laboratories. It is nature and the chemist combined.

"It is that which has been spoken of as possible by some and laughed at by others. It is the product of a cross-fertilisation of the wild fibre plants and the cotton plant. Who was it discovered it?

"Ah, I remember! It was a German scientist. With their usual secrecy, they have persevered in it. How long they have been working upon it, one can't say. But that they have produced a commercial possibility is proved. And that brings me to the green cotton blossoms which appeared so mysteriously at the Trott factory.

"I wonder what Morris would say if I told him his purple blooms had never been stolen, nor had they ever been removed from the cases? He would probably think I was mad. But it is so.

"The one thousand dozen cheap cotton blooms which puzzle him so were once the same number of silken blooms. And I am probably the only man in London who realises it. But stay! There is another who knows—the one who caused that change."

Blake's jaws came together with a snap, and he swung back to the experimenting table. With infinite care he picked up the piece of purple silk, and with a pair of scissors evened the end from which he had been cutting samples. Then he creased the piece exactly in the middle. That done, he laid it out flat on the table, and over one half of it placed a large sheet of glass, the edge of which ran along the crease he had made.

Now he refilled the spray with the colourless liquid from the small bottle, and with a steady hand, sprayed the half which was not under the glass. He watched it closely while it went through the various changes in colour until it remained fixed at green.

Then he removed the piece of glass which had protected the other half from the vapour, and held up what was indeed a piece of strange material. Half of it was rich, shimmering purple, half was sickly, sheenless green.

What a contrast they made! One of silk, one of cotton. Yet the peculiar thing was that it still appeared to be one piece of cloth. And so it was. Not one man in a hundred thousand could have explained it.

Blake folded it up, and laid it to one side, together with the green blooms, and the length of wire; then he went back to the consulting-room. Barely had he reached it, when the door opened abruptly, and there entered a florid-looking man of elderly aspect. At the present moment he was obviously very upset, and his close-cropped, white side-whiskers fairly bristled with indignation. Blake regarded him quietly.

"Might I inquire—" he began.

"I beg your pardon for entering in this way," spluttered the other, growing somewhat calmer under Blake's quiet gaze. "Are you Mr. Blake? But I know you are, I recognise you from your pictures!"

"Then perhaps you will tell me who you are, and why you have come?" suggested Blake.

The other sat down heavily.

"I am Sir Hector Trott."

"Ah! Have you come to see me about the strange occurrence at your factory, Sir Hector?"

"Eh? Oh, no! I had forgotten about that. I have come to see you about a far more serious matter, Mr. Blake. The most valuable horse I own has disappeared, and I want you to find him."

Blake sat down at his desk, and leaned forward.

"The most valuable horse you own has disappeared! You have several, Sir Hector. Which one is gone?"

"Sunset. I only bought him a few days ago."

"I know the horse. I read about your purchase of him. Let me see—you paid, I think, twenty thousand for him?"

"That was the figure. I bought him for the stud, and now he is gone!"

"Supposing you tell me the facts, Sir Hector."

"There isn't much to tell. I received a message over the 'phone from the steward of my country place, saying the horse had disappeared from the paddock, he was put out as usual yesterday in a small grass paddock kept specially for him.

"The stable-boy went to get him in the afternoon, to lead him back to the stable for the night. When he reached the paddock it was empty. Thinking the gate may have become unfastened in some way, he examined it. It had not been touched, as far as he could see.

"There were some mares in a small paddock adjoining, and his next thought was that the stallion had jumped the fence. You know he was a fine jumper. But he wasn't there.

"The boy became frightened, and carried the news back to the trainer. He in turn notified the steward, and they set up a search. Well, to make a long story short, they didn't notify me at once because they thought they should soon find him. They scouted the countryside, but couldn't find a trace of him.

"But here is the funny part of the thing, and is what makes me think he has been stolen. A man who lives near—a small farmer says he was coming along the road near the paddock yesterday afternoon, when he saw one of those motor-vans for shifting horses standing not far away from the gate.

"He didn't think anything of it at the time, because they are fairly common now. He merely thought some horse was going to be taken to a hunt meeting. But about twenty minutes after the motor-truck passed his place, driving at a rapid pace. Of course, he couldn't see if there was a horse inside.

"All that I got over the 'phone from the steward. It may mean something, or it may be a pure coincidence. But it seems funny that it should be pulled up near Sunset's paddock, and that shortly after the horse should be missing.

"This is a serious matter, Mr. Blake, and I want you to take it on at once, will you? I don't want the horse to fall into the hands of people who may maim him."

"But I am already on another matter," said Blake.

"You mean that trouble at the factory?"

"Yes."

"Let that go! It is of no importance compared to the loss of the horse."

"You don't, by any chance, connect the two, do you?"

"Good heavens! No! Do you?"

"I shouldn't care to say yet, Sir Hector. But I shall certainly look into the disappearance of the horse."

"Thank you. I am going down to my place in the country to-night. Will you come with me?"

Blake shook his head.

"I must ask you to excuse me. I wish to attend to one of two things here to-night. I shall, however, motor through in the morning. By the way, where is your place?"

"Bishop's Manor, just outside Horton in Surrey. Anyone can direct you."

"Very well. I shall be down in the morning."

"I shall be there to meet you, and you can go right into the matter. I don't think you will find any connection between the disappearance of Sunset and that affair at the factory, Mr. Blake. I imagine some horse people are behind this thing."

"Perhaps!" remarked Blake, as he rose.

A moment later the door had closed behind Sir Hector, and Blake was just reaching for his pipe, when Tinker appeared. He tossed his cap to one side, and laid a slip of paper on the desk.

"Well?" queried Blake.

"I went to the address on the paper, sir," replied the lad. "I asked about 'Miss Craig.' It was a boarding establishment, you thought, but they had never heard tell of 'Miss Craig.'"

"I was afraid not," grunted Blake, as his fingers closed on his pipe.

YVONNE HOLDS UP THE MOTOR CAR!

Yvonne whipped out a small revolver of her own and pointed it full at the infuriated owner of the car.
"Fetch Alan to bind this man up!" she said sharply to Hendricks.

U. J.—No. 573.

"THE CASE OF THE GERMAN TRADER" NEXT WEEK!

AFTER her coup at the factory of the Trott Manufacturing Co., Yvonne had by no means been idle. As she herself had remarked on her return, the punishment of Sir Hector Trott was not complete. Nor was it.

During the month she had spent at the factory as typist, she had acquired much information about the baronet's affairs. She had studied his pet schemes and hobbies; she knew what his engagements were for some time ahead; she had followed his movements with a zest which would have surprised him considerably had he known.

She knew about the purchase of Sunset, and the price paid by the papers. That was before she had launched out upon her campaign. And she knew all about the subsequent movements of the famous horse.

She had a thorough acquaintance with Bishop's Manor, and the arrangement of its personnel. That a special paddock had been allotted for Sunset was well known to her, and the fact that the baronet's country place was a bare dozen miles from her own was the means of her conceiving a further brilliant coup in her campaign. She would steal Sunset.

Once she made up her mind to this, she moved with her usual directness. A telegram had been sent to the Fleur-de-Lys, ordering Hendricks, the mate, to come on to Surrey, and to bring half a dozen of the sailors with him.

That had been three days before her coup at the factory on Saturday night. On Sunday, even before she had arisen, they had arrived from London. In the garage reposed a large motor horse-van, relic of the other period of her residence there. Alec had been put to work upon this, and now its engine ran sweetly.

At two o'clock. Alec, with Hendricks beside him, had driven away, and it is safe to say that any who witnessed the passage of the van never dreamed two able-bodied men were concealed inside it.

An hour later, they had reached the paddock where Sunset was grazing. There they were compelled to move with circumspection.

First a loaded motor swept past them; then a lone farmer appeared trudging along. That was the man who later reported having seen them. When he had passed they risked a move. While Alec released the two men inside the van, Hendricks moved along to the

63

gate bearing a measure of oats. Sunset was standing in the very centre of the paddock, his head raised in kingly disdain. But then he hadn't seen the oats.

Hard on Hendricks' heels came Alec and the other two, one of whom bore a strong halter rope. Leaning over the gate, Hendricks whistled softly, and rattled the oats, allowing the breeze to pick up some of them and blow them along in the direction of the stallion.

Slowly his head came round, and he sniffed. Then he took a step forward, and sniffed again. Curveting gracefully, he began to approach. Hendricks now took out a handful, and let them fall at his feet.

Sunset's conquest was complete. He came forward daintily, and nosed the oats on the ground; then he lifted his head, and went for the measure. Hendricks let him get a good mouthful, then he breathed:

"Now!"

From behind the gate rose the seaman who held the halter rope, and before the stallion could gather what was happening, it had been slipped over his head, imprisoning him. He reared dangerously, but on the instant the other seaman was over the gate, soothing him.

A moment later he was calm, nibbling contentedly at the oats while Alec worked at the padlock which fastened the gate.

It was by no means an intricate form of lock, and the master key with which Yvonne had provided him soon had it hanging loose.

Then the gate was cautiously opened, and, lured by the oats Sunset was led through. Motor-vans held no terrors for the stallion, for he had often travelled in them before. A motor-van it had been which brought him down to his present quarters.

He baulked a little at the start, but when Hendricks entered with the oats, he followed docilely enough. Then he was secured, the two seamen remaining inside with him. Hendricks slipped out past him, and closed the door, resuming his place on the front seat.

Alec had been busy refastening the gate and destroying the marks made, but now he finished, and hurried up. Shortly after, the van was speeding homewards with its precious prize!

Now, Yvonne knew perfectly well the disappearance of the stallion would create an uproar at Bishop's Manor, and she reckoned on the baronet being sent for post haste. She also calculated that every effort would be made to recover the horse at once, and not to let the news of the occurrence leak out to the public unless it were necessary.

Therefore, she figured that Sir Hector would arrive at his country place not later than Sunday night.

In that supposition she was mistaken. She had not taken into account the possibility of the employees at the estate endeavouring to find the horse at once, and so conceal the affair even from the baronet. They knew perfectly well that someone of them, or possibly all of them, would be the recipient of his wrath if he knew, and consequently they wished to avoid that if possible.

By narrow by-ways and lanes, Yvonne, heavily veiled, motored over that evening, and had Alec draw up the car in a quiet spot. While she remained in the car, he went scouting and, by joining a party of stable boys from the manor, managed to elicit the information that the baronet had not yet been notified.

They had taken him merely for the chauffeur of a neighbouring estate anxious to help, and had freely aired their anxiety in his presense. Then he had returned to the car, and reported to Yvonne.

She shrugged at the news.

"I hadn't counted on that, Alec," she said knitting her brows. "It means they fear his anger, and will not notify him until they have searched high and low. They will probably look further afield to-morrow, and when they fail will, as a last revert, inform Sir Hector. We can do nothing more to-night. Get in and drive back home."

But the next morning, Yvonne sent for Alec.

"Motor over to Bishop's Manor again, Alec," she ordered. "Leave the car some place, and join one of the search parties. Your presence will cause no comment, for half the people in the neighbourhood will be hunting about.

"They can't keep the occurrence quiet any longer, though they may conceal the name of the horse. Stay there until you find out what has been done about informing Sir Hector Trott. As soon as you know, come and report."

Alec had lost no time in obeying her commands, and on arriving had left his car in the yard of a farmer. Then he had trudged along until he picked up the same party of lads with whom he had been the previous day.

All afternoon he was compelled to tramp about the country searching for the horse he knew they had no possibility of finding. It was close on six when they were joined by another lad from the stable, who brought the news that Sir Hector had been sent for and would be down that night.

Thenceforth the efforts of the search party were redoubled, and in the excitement, Alec managed to slip away without being noticed. Reaching the car by a roundabout way, he jumped in and drove homewards at top speed. On arriving there he reported at once to Yvonne, and immediately preparations were made for another coup— a coup which Yvonne had planned as the last and crowning move in the present campaign.

Just before dusk the big car swung down the elm-lined drive. In the front seat sat Alec, bending over the wheel; in the tonneau was Yvonne, wrapped about by a heavy cloak and rug. At the bottom of the tonneau lay Hendricks and one of the seamen invisible to the eyes of passers-by.

Alec drove on steadily until Bishop's Manor was passed, and good three miles more had been covered. Then he drew up and worked the car into the shadow of the overhanging hedges. Yvonne descended at once, and strode on for about two hundred yards, where she sat down and waited.

From where she was, her own car was invisible. Alec had risked extinguishing the lights. Hendricks and the sailor still lay in the bottom of the tonneau.

It was perfectly dark now with no moon. A bank of heavy clouds hid the stars, and lent a lone, dreary atmosphere to the spot.

The minutes passed slowly, mounting well up to the half hour before any sound broke the stillness. The strained senses of the watchers recognised it at once as the distant purr of a motor. Louder and louder it grew, until suddenly two brilliant headlights swept into view, and a big car thundered down upon Yvonne.

She raised herself and leaned forward, watching for something. Then the lights swept past, and she saw a single occupant in the front seat. It disappeared from view a moment later. It was not the car for which she was looking.

Another ten minutes passed before the silence was again broken. This time a motor cyclist swept past, and almost at once there followed a small runabout bearing two people.

Silence for a quarter of an hour, then low on the night air came the song or a powerful engine. Yvonne leaned forward eagerly as the lights swept into view. It way level with her in no time, and as it went past, she saw it contained two occupants. One was the driver; the other was a passenger in the tonneau.

As her eyes took in the latter, she hastily raised her hand, and applied something to her lips. Immediately a loud whistle rent the air, rising even above the noise of the car; then she sprang into the road and raced along.

As she ran, she saw a red light being swung to and fro, heard the grinding of the brakes as the big car was brought up short, heard the sound of a sharp, angry voice, then she was upon the scene.

In the very middle of the road stood the car which had just passed. Standing up in the tonneau and speaking angrily was an elderly man with short side whiskers. Yvonne realised with a smile of satisfaction that her fleeting recognition had been correct. It was Sir Hector Trott, furious.

And from his point of view he had cause to be. Standing close to the car was a big nautical-looking man who held a heavy automatic pointing steadily at the baronet's heart. Another man was keeping the driver covered, while a third was busy at a car which stood in the shadow at the side of the road.

Yvonne lowered her veil, and stepped forward. From her pocket she took a small revolver, and trained it on the baronet.

"Tell Alec to bind him at once," she said in low tones, and Hendricks who had been the cause of Sir Hector's wrath, lowered his revolver to obey.

Despite the threats and protests of the baronet, they not only bound and gagged him, but blindfolded him as well. When he was trussed up to their satisfaction, they deposited him in the tonneau of his own car, and turned their attention to the driver whom the sailor had been keeping covered. He received the same attention as the baronet, and was laid beside his master in the tonneau.

At Yvonne's command, Alec climbed into the front seat, and took the wheel. The sailor entered the tonneau, and sat over the victims, a revolver on the seat beside him. Yvonne took the wheel of her own car and motioned to Hendricks to sit beside her.

Then Alec drove off followed by Yvonne, and so the two cars thundered along the Surrey roads towards the old Tudor place which was Yvonne's.

BLAKE had had a strong reason for not accompanying Sir Hector Trott to Bishop's Manor. His motive had been a desire to apply a solid analysis to the problem in hand, for, ever since his startling discovery during the examination of the silk, a vague uneasiness had been stirring his mind.

At one stroke he had eliminated every possible suspect of a certain class. No ordinary individual had been capable of carrying out such an intricate coup against the Trott Manufacturing Co. It had been the product of a mind well versed in the very latest scientific problems, and where before the circle of suspicion had included many possibilities, it now resolved itself into a narrow ring enclosing but few likely suspects.

Blake was by no means blind to the fact that business rivalry might have inspired the deed. He knew perfectly well that many strange things were done in the game of big business, and during his career had come across things which outdid the wildest realms of romance. Such had been his first idea, and this he had been pondering on when Sir Hector Trott had burst in to announce the disappearance of Sunset.

That evening Blake felt a need to dissect the whole case, and so when dinner was over, he sought the consulting-room. Filling his pipe he sank into the easy chair which had seen the solution of so many complex problems, and, closing his eyes, sent his mind into the maze contained within the mental "circle" he had drawn.

Somewhere in that mass were two facts for which he was probing as the surgeon probes the wound. *Motive*—the other was *Instrument*.

The why of the affair might be traced, once the instrument—in this case a highly scientific human instrument—were discovered. Or vice versa once the motive was found, the instrument could be deduced.

Was it the outcome of business jealousy? Certainly a silk firm with German connections might well be the instrument in the case. Motive with them would be plain.

For instance, supposing a Continental firm with a branch in London had so far held a monopoly of the silk business of Jarridge's, they would not easily let go of such a profitable account.

When they found that the Trott Co. was poaching on their

preserves they may have sought to discredit the London firm at one blow. And certainly there was little question about the success of that blow, whoever had struck it.

Did the case begin there and end there, Blake would have felt strongly inclined to follow up that supposition until it either led him to the goal or a blank wall. But there was more to be considered. He did not hold with Sir Hector Trott that the silk outrage and the disappearance of Sunset were the work of two separate and distinct sources, having two separate and distinct motives.

The nearness of the events and the coincidence of their mysterious suddenness was too strong a factor to be disregarded. He did not think for a moment that the stallion had jumped the fence and wandered away of his own accord.

Stallions of the cut of Sunset do not wander about the roads of a thickly settled county without being seen by dozens of people. And if the steward's telephonic report which the baronet had repeated were to be trusted the horse had not been seen by a single soul.

Again there was the incident of the motor horse-van seen standing near the paddock by a passing farmer. That was too suspicions a circumstance, preceding the disappearance of the stallion, to be dismissed from the affair.

In fact, so suggestive was it that in the absence of a personal investigation at Bishop's Manor, Blake looked upon it as the strongest clue in the matter.

But there the circle swung round again to the outrage at the factory. Presuming the one who committed that needed to possess a certain scientific knowledge, which was an undoubted fact, then the instigator of the theft of Sunset must also be of more than ordinary intelligence.

And wasn't the stealing of the famous stallion in broad daylight the result of a daring and methodical mind? Its success proved that no point had been overlooked. Its daring was not the clumsy courage of the amateur, but the cool calculation of the artist.

More and more as his deduction progressed, Blake labelled the two occurrences due to one and the same source. Then what was the motive?

Was it a second outrage by business rivals? Where the spoiling of the silk order smacked strongly of such a source, the disappearance of the horse weakened that supposition.

Once a rival firm had succeeded in ruining the silken blooms their purpose would have been effected. It would serve them nothing to add to the stroke, and would only arouse more inquiry, a thing which they would not be anxious to court.

Then there was the odd circumstance of Morris' typist. Certainly there was nothing suspicious in a typist only remaining at work a month, but, when a typist gives an address at which she is totally unknown, then there is something fishy in it.

Who was this "Miss Craig" who went to work at the Trott manufactory about two weeks after they had received the silk order from Jarridge's? Why had she given notice on the very day when Morris had dictated a letter to Jarridge's informing them that the order would be delivered in a week's time?

It wasn't as though one of the other typists had given notice, but she had been Morris' typist. *She had written that letter.* She had left on the day the silk order was completed. And between the time of her leaving and the delivery of the order on Monday morning the blooms had been ruined.

Nor was it hard for Blake to fix the time of the outrage. He hadn't the slightest doubt but that it had been carried out Saturday night. The long sleep of the watchman was too suspicious a circumstance to be overlooked. That sleep had been no accidental doze. It had been the result of cleverness far in advance to any such germs possessed by the watchman. Of that Blake was certain.

Then was the mysterious "Miss Craig," the spy of rival silk interests? Had she been placed in the Trott factory in order to get certain information? And when she had got it, had she reported to her real employers?

Or—and here is where the vague uneasiness stirred Blake's mind—had she been acting on her own? If she were—if she had no employers, but was the instrument of her own plans— then there was only one conclusion possible. "Miss Craig" was no ordinary typist. She was no ordinary woman.

On the contrary, she must be a remarkable individual altogether—learned, cool, calm, deliberating, methodical, and possessed of an indomitable will to carry out her purpose.

Moreover, she must be possessed of unbounded resources, of which money was far from the more important. She must have provided a perfect retreat. The perfection of the deed at the factory, proved that.

Then who was there who could fill these conditions? She must be young, more than ordinarily clever, wealthy, have large resources behind her, possess a high degree of scientific knowledge, be more than ordinarily good looking, and have the cool courage to carry out her purpose.

Morris had described her as having "red hair." And that description was the keynote of Blake's uneasiness. He knew perfectly well that, to a man like Morris, all hair of a certain shade was red. But Blake knew himself a girl who fulfilled all the above conditions, and whose hair was like burnished copper.

And what increased his foreboding was that he remembered vividly a conversation he had held, some months before, regarding the cross-fertilisation of the wild fibre plants of Central America with the cotton plant, in order to produce a substitute for silk.

For once in his life Sexton Blake was angry with his memory. For the first time during his career he felt that he would like to toss up a case. For the first time *he did not want* to find his quarry.

And why? He couldn't have told himself. He only knew that all those rigid conditions fitted perfectly to the personality of Mademoiselle Yvonne.

Not yet had he forgotten his futile visit to Queen Anne's Gate a little over a month ago. Yet, had he gazed upon a certain letter which he had read many, many times during that month, he might have found an answer.

Sexton Blake was a methodical machine in the solution of the most baffling problems when they concerned other people. He was a blind man when he came to his own feelings.

He didn't realise yet that a war was being waged within him. He didn't realise that Yvonne's dear, whimsical personality had invaded the innermost recesses of his being. He did know that her going out of his life had hurt as things had never before hurt. But he didn't analyse the feeling. He couldn't.

Yet within him the combatants in that war were his own unblemished heart and his stern sense of duty. Time might dull the pain of the loss and hard work bring forgetfulness. But if things were to arise such as had arisen, bringing suggestions of Yvonne, and pointing to her as the breaker of laws, what should he do? What could he do?

Though it must hurt as nothing had ever hurt, he knew that in any event he would do his duty. Such was the man as a man self-immolated to duty.

It was long past midnight when he rose and wearily sought his room. The final result of his pondering had been a decision to look into the possibility of a rival silk firm having instigated the outrage, and to endeavour to discover if the mysterious "Miss Craig" had been but a tool of theirs.

Then, if that led to nothing, he would endeavour to apply the connection of the disappearance of Sunset with the affair of the factory. Should that, in turn, prove abortive, then only one thing remained to be done. He must follow the arrow of his suspicions.

It was past eight when he awoke. As he opened his eyes he realised that it was Tinker's voice which had wakened him. The lad seemed to be talking over the telephone with someone, and a moment later, when Blake heard him say, "Just a minute, please; I will see if he can come," he knew it was a call for him.

Tinker appeared a moment later.

"You are wanted on the 'phone, guv'nor. Can you come?"

"Who is it, Tinker?" asked Blake irritably.

"Mr. Morris, sir. He seems in a great way, too. Says he must speak to you at once."

Blake rose at once and slipped on a dressing-gown. Then he went along to the consulting-room. Seating himself at the desk, he picked up the receiver which lay on the blotting-pad.

"Hello!" he called. "This is Sexton Blake speaking."

"This is Morris, Mr. Blake."

"Yes; what is it, Mr. Morris? Any new developments?"

"I should say so. Did you hear about Sunset being stolen?"

"Oh, yes! Sir Hector was here yesterday afternoon, and told me. He went down last night, and I promised to go down to-day. Is that all?"

"No. Sir Hector left London last night, Mr. Blake. He started for Bishop's Manor, his country place in Surrey. But he never arrived. He, the chauffeur, and the car have completely disappeared!"

IF Blake had any hesitancy to push forward on the present investigation, it was effectually killed by the startling words of the manager. In those few words, what had been one strong possibility in the case was settled for ever. No rival silk firm had carried things as far as that. The cause must be looked for in a different direction.

Little could be gained by discussing the last occurrence over the 'phone, so asking Morris to come on to Baker Street without delay, Blake rang off. He dressed hurriedly and breakfasted at once.

Then he made his way to the laboratory and picked up the bi-coloured piece of cloth, which was now half silk and half cotton. Returning to the consulting-room, he laid it on the desk and seated himself.

Next he opened a drawer of the desk, and from it look a photograph. He held it in his hand, and gazed upon it with a strange expression in his eyes; then, with a tightening of the lips, he placed it on the desk in such a position that it must be seen by anyone sitting opposite him.

Scarcely had he done so when a knock came at the door, and Mrs. Bardell announced "Mr. Morris." The manager followed on her heels, and advanced across the room with hurried strides. His face was lined with worry, and his first words showed what was uppermost in his mind.

"Well, Mr. Blake, what do you think of this latest development? I—"

Blake held up his hand.

"Wait, Mr. Morris. Sit down, please. Let us get at the facts properly. Since I know of the disappearance of the horse Sunset, we can leave that for the moment. Tell me as briefly as possible what you know about Sir Hector."

"There isn't much to tell, Mr. Blake. I had barely reached the office this morning when the 'phone rang. It was Grant, the steward of Sir Hector's place in Surrey. He wanted to know if Sir Hector had changed his plans about going down. I said I knew nothing of the matter, and that he should ring up the house.

"About fifteen minutes later, Lady Trott called up, and told me that he had left for Surrey the previous evening. The steward has seen nothing of him or the car. If it hadn't been for the fact that his horse had been stolen, I should have thought little about it. He might have changed his plans and gone to some place else for the night.

"But it looked too suspicious. The steward was all for calling in the police, but I choked him off. I know that is the last thing Sir Hector would wish. He has a horror of notoriety. Still, unless something can be done immediately, I shall have to notify Scotland Yard."

"I hope that will not be necessary, Mr. Morris. In fact, I may say, since yesterday I have made several investigations, and I have a strong suspicion into whose hands Sir Hector has fallen. Er—what is the matter?"

Blake asked the question as he saw a look of profound amazement steal over the face of the manager. He was gazing intently at the photograph which Blake had placed on the desk. At the latter's words he looked up.

"That—that photograph!" he jerked, "It is the dead likeness of Miss Craig!"

"So?" remarked Blake carelessly. "That is the likeness of a friend. By the way, I have something to show you."

Though he spoke casually, Blake's tones by no means indicated his inner feelings. Morris's remark had sent a wave of depression over him, for his test had proved itself, and now he knew that his deduction had not been wrong. Still, he had no intention of permitting Morris to know yet.

Whatever he may have felt, politeness forbade the manager referring further to the photograph, though his puzzled gaze returned to it again and again. In the meantime, Blake was unfolding the bi-coloured piece of cloth, and now he spread it out before the manager.

"Just have a look at that, and tell me what you think of it," said Blake quietly.

Morris picked up the goods and bent his gaze upon the line where rich purple and tawdry green met.

"I don't understand, Mr. Blake," he said. "Where did you get a piece of this green? It is the same from which the green blooms were made. And how on earth did you get it joined to the silk as it is? It is the most masterly piece of weaving I have ever seen."

"It ought to be," replied Blake. "It was not joined on. It is part of the same piece. But come with me, Mr. Morris. I can see you do not credit the fact."

74

He rose and conducted the manager along the passage to the laboratory. Approaching the experimenting-table, he laid the piece of cloth down und took up a small syringe, then he reached down the small bottle of colourless liquid and filled the spray.

That done, he drew across the sheet of glass which he had previously used, and once more arranged it over the cloth. This time only a quarter of the length was protected. Projecting beyond was an equal portion of purple silk and the full half of green cotton.

Morris watched in puzzled silence while Blake took up the spray and saturated the exposed portion of purple silk with the white vapour. As it slowly paled in colour, running up the scale of colours until it remained fixed at the sickly green shade, he drew a deep breath of amazement.

Blake turned to him with a faint smile.

"Mr. Morris," he said, "you acknowledge that a few moments ago, the portion which has just changed colour was silk, do you not?"

"Certainly, Mr. Blake."

"Then, let me ask you to examine that same bit under the glass. You are an experienced judge of materials, so should be able to tell me what it is."

As he spoke, Blake was busy arranging the microscope, and putting beneath the lens a portion of the cloth. Then he motioned to the manager.

"It is ready. Have a look and tell me what you see."

Morris bent over immediately and placed his eye to the eye-piece. He gazed long and steadily, breathing with rising emotion as he did so. Suddenly he lifted his head and swung on to Blake.

"Mr. Blake," he cried, "I don't know how you have done it, but you have changed that portion of silk to cotton!"

"Let us return to the consulting-room, Mr. Morris; I will explain."

They made their way back, and when they were again seated, Blake explained in detail how the chemical change had been effected and why it did re-act to the treatment where pure silk would not have done so.

"It was the colour test which revealed the secret," he said in conclusion. "The vapour not only acted on the dye, but destroyed the wild fibre in the cloth, leaving the cotton base.

"And that brings us back to the case. I presume you see now that the blooms which were sent to Jarridge's were the same which had entered your factory as blooms of purple silk.

"Each lot was treated in the fashion you have just seen. Consequently, when they were delivered they had apparently been replaced by cotton creations.

"It also tells you something else, Mr. Morris. It proves that no dishonest employee was responsible for the deed. Such a change was far beyond the ordinary individual.

"Now, when Sir Hector Trott was here yesterday, he scouted the idea that there was any connection between the outrage at the factory and the disappearance of the horse, Sunset. I disagreed with him then, and, since hearing the news regarding him, my belief is still stronger that the three deeds are the work of one and the same source."

"When I came in you said you had suspicions," put in the manager. "I didn't mention it yesterday, but we have a bitter rival here in London—The Swift Silk Co. Do you think they could be behind this thing?"

"No. I considered that fully last night. If the affair had begun and ended with the spoiling of the flowers, it would have been a reasonable theory. Their motive might easily be to nip in the bud any connections you were making with Jarridge's.

"But the two subsequent occurrences make it impossible for me to entertain that theory. Don't you see that the whole affair is on a much bigger scale than business rivalry?

"The disappearance of the horse shows a desire to strike at Sir Hector Trott personally. And the fact that he himself is now missing but strengthens that. Still the blooms have a strong place in the case, and if they were not the chief object of the attack, which I can't believe they were, then in my opinion, *they had some very strong connection with the reason.*

"In other words, when we find out why the flowers were ruined we will discover the motive for the whole thing. By the way, when you first outlined what had happened, you said they were all made by out-workers."

"Yes."

"Would it be possible that those workers were strongly dissatisfied with the conditions of work? How much do you pay?"

"Ordinarily, ninepence a dozen."

"That tells me little. How many would a worker make in a day?"

76

"Two to three dozen."

"Ah! Not a very heavy income, is it?"

"It is what the other factories pay," replied Morris a trifle stiffly.

Blake was silent, thinking. Unconsciously his gaze was resting upon Yvonne's photograph. He was pondering over the manager's last words, and somewhere in his mind was a persistent thought of Yvonne.

Was it possible that something connected with those blooms had caused her to attack Sir Hector Trott as she had done? For, since the manager's recognition of her likeness to Miss Craig the last ramparts of doubts had fallen in Blake's mind. He knew somehow that Yvonne was the culprit. He was roused by the other's voice.

"About Sir Hector, Mr. Blake."

"Ah! yes," responded Blake. "We must find him at once. Would you care to come down to Surrey with me? I shall leave at once."

"You think you will get traces of him there?"

"I think we shall find him there," answered Blake quietly.

"Then I should like to go down with you."

"Very well, I shall send for the car at once."

As he spoke, Blake rang for Tinker, and when the lad put in an appearance ordered him to 'phone the garage. A few minutes later, the car was chugging at the kerb outside and they prepared to leave. Blake took the wheel, and beside him sat the chauffeur, Davis. In the back were Tinker, Pedro and the manager.

Why Blake retained the chauffeur and took Tinker and Pedro, Morris had no idea. But he presumed the detective had his own reasons and so said nothing. He did not know that Davis, the chauffeur, was an ex-middleweight champion boxer; and, if he had, he would have been none the wiser.

They drove straight through to Bishop's Manor, making the estate under the two hours. The steward met them on their arrival, and conducted them to his office, there telling Blake all he knew about the disappearance of the horse and the baronet.

The facts of the former were, in substance, the same as those related to Blake by Sir Hector himself. The steward was only able to add that the search was still in progress and that so far they had discovered nothing.

About Sir Hector's fate he knew very little. He had expected the baronet the previous evening, and when he had not come thought something had detained him. He had telephoned in the morning, and was told that the baronet had left in the car arranged. Somewhere between London and Bishop's Manor he had disappeared and with him had gone both the chauffeur and car.

Blake listened in silence to the story, then he spoke.

"I should like to talk with the farmer who saw the motor horse-van standing on the road, Sunday," he said. "Will you have him sent for. He can meet us at the paddock. I should like to go there at once."

"Certainly," replied the steward. "I will have a stable-boy ride over at once and tell him."

"How far is the paddock where Sunset was kept?" asked Blake.

"About half a mile."

"Then we may as well walk."

They all rose and made their way outside. While the steward went to see about sending a stable-lad for the farmer, Blake drew Tinker aside.

"Listen, Tinker," he said in low tones; "do you remember the case we had involving Cornelius Patterson, the Canadian millionaire?" [2]

"Yes, guv'nor."

"Then you will remember that our search after the diamond involved in that case brought us to Surrey."

"Why, yes, sir. We traced it to Mademoiselle Yvonne. Patterson was one of the men who had had a hand in financially ruining her and her mother in Australia."

"Exactly, my lad. The excellence of your memory saves me going into detail. You will remember, then, to where we finally traced it?"

"Yes, sir, to the estate which Yvonne had down here."

"Quite right. Well, my lad, this place is about ten miles from the village of Horton. Mademoiselle Yvonne's place is about two miles the other side of Horton. I know that she hasn't occupied it for months and that it has been leased.

"But at the same time, I want you to motor over to Horton. Leave the car there and go ahead on foot. Before you do so, go into a quiet spot in the woods and alter your appearance somewhat. The more you look like a country lad the better. Scout about the place, and find out

---

2 See UNION JACK, No. 501; "The Detective Airman."
(available in Stillwoods Edition. /drf)

what you can. I am anxious to know if Yvonne is occupying it at present."

"Scott! Is she mixed up in this thing, sir? I thought she had given up all—"

"That will do, Tinker," interrupted Blake sternly. "You will understand things better when you see the outcome of the case. Return here as soon as possible. I am keen to get that information quickly."

"All right, sir. I'll go at once."

The lad hurried over to the car and climbed in, muttering as he did so:

"Scott! but the guv'nor was touchy when I spoke of Yvonne. I wonder what has happened to stir him up like that."

He little knew of the long hours of struggle Blake had gone through the previous evening.

The steward appeared just as Tinker drove off, and the party started across the fields for the small paddock where Sunset had been kept. On reaching it Blake took a long look round it.

"No horse ever jumped those barriers," he grunted briefly. "Let us go over to the gate."

They trooped across to the high gate and found the farmer had arrived. One by one they climbed over and dropped to the other side. The farmer touched his cap.

"You are the man who saw a motor horse-van standing near here, are you not?" asked Blake.

"Yes, sir."

"Will you point out to me exactly where it stood? No! Don't go to show me. Point out from here."

Blake glanced along the lane to where a tree threw its branches over the hedgerow. Then, requesting the others to remain where they were, he walked forward alone. Since Sunday, the ground had been, trampled and cut by the feet of many horses and men for, from that point, most of the searchers had started. At first glance there seemed little likelihood of finding any distinctive marks, but there was always a possibility.

On reaching the spot Blake dropped to his knees and drawing out his pocket-glass bent even lower. Foot by foot he went over the ground before him, searching patiently for the sign which he sought. Finally, in the medley of marks before him he saw it—the remaining impression of a heavy tyre.

From that he worked back. Presuming it to be the rear wheel, then the particular thing for which he was in search ought to be a few feet behind it.

Now he started in a most peculiar fashion. Instead of examining the ground as he had been doing he began going over it crosswise in long parallel lines about five feet from where he imagined the rear of the van to have been. That was a good seven feet back of the wheel marks allowing for the body to project about two feet beyond the rear axle.

He worked with extreme patience, moving in lines scarcely an inch apart. In length, they were governed by the average width of a van. The party back at the gate could not fathom his purpose. It had been plain enough at first that he was searching for the marks of the tires, but why he should be examining the ground seven feet back, they could not guess. And when he finally rose with a grunt they did not know even then what he had found. He walked back to them slowly.

"It is quite useless for you to search the countryside on the chance that the stallion wandered away of his own accord," he said addressing the steward. "He was taken in the motor van which stood near here."

"Why, how do you know that?" asked the steward in amazement.

"Very simple. In order to get him into the van they lowered a board incline which ran from the rear of the van to the ground. The height of the van would make a length of about five feet necessary, in order that the incline should not be too steep.

"Running across the road are the remains of the line caused by the affair resting upon it. And just this side of it are several hoof-marks pointing towards it, showing that the horse baulked a little before going up.

"They are too close to the line, and the direction in which they point too suggestive, to think that they are the casual hoof-prints of a horse belonging to one of the search party. But if the stallion was taken through the gate further proof should be easy to procure. One moment, until I examine the padlock."

Bending as he spoke, Blake applied his glass to the lock, and studied it closely for some minutes. At last he raised his head.

"As I thought," he said briefly. "It has been opened by a key which did not belong to the lock. There are very few marks, but enough for the purpose."

Then he turned to Morris.

"As I said in London, Mr. Morris, the stallion is a victim of a deliberate plot. The same source which succeeded in spiriting him away is that which has caused Sir Hector's disappearance.

"When we find the horse we will find Sir Hector, or traces of him. I have a very strong suspicion where that may be, but I cannot tell definitely until the return of my assistant. He is now following up a certain clue.

"From his report I shall know whether we will make a move in that direction or not. If we do, it will be to-night. Until then there is nothing more to be done. Let us return to the house and wait."

And, wonderingly, they trooped along beside him, consumed with curiosity but not daring to break through Blake's reserve.

WHEN Tinker got away from Bishop's Manor he picked up the main road which passed through Horton, and sent the car along at high speed. It was only ten miles, and the big machine ate them up in less than twenty-five minutes.

He eased up as he neared the village, for he had had a previous experience with the trap for motorists which was usually set close to it. As he drove sedately along the single main street he grinned to himself as he saw a constable regarding him suspiciously.

He made for the inn where he and Blake had stopped before, and, leaving the car in the yard, struck off on foot without delay, he knew a quiet copse by the roadside not far out, and for there he was bound.

As he reached it he looked carefully up and down the road, and, seeing no one in sight, took the fence at a single bound. He trotted on until he was within the shelter of the trees, then went to work to change his appearance.

His first procedure was to sit down and unlace his boots. Then he tucked the bottom of his trousers inside and laced them up again. Following that he divested himself of his tie and collar, rolling them up and stuffing them in his pocket.

Now he loosened his shirt at the throat, and next took off his coat. By the simple expedient of turning it inside out he was in possession of a jacket which looked decidedly the worse for wear. A good many of Tinker's garments were made for a quick change, a circumstance which had stood him in good stead on more than one occasion.

When he had ruffled his hair, drawn his cap down carelessly and begrimed his hands with earth, he looked an entirely different individual from the spruce young chap who had entered Horton in a motor half an hour before. Should any doubt it let them follow the same procedure. They will be surprised at the result.

When at last he was ready he made his way to a tiny stream which trickled close at hand, and inspected himself in that limpid mirror of Nature.

"You may not look the ideal farm lad," he grinned at his reflection, "but you certainly don't look like the person you really are. I guess it will serve the purpose all right."

Straightening himself he started off through the copse until he reached a clearing which mounted to a low hill. He trudged up it until he could get a view of his immediate surroundings, then, when he had his bearings, started off towards the left.

Through field and wood he trudged steadily until he reached a high park fence stretching away to right and left. At its foot he paused.

"If I am not mistaken, this is the place," he murmured. "I seem to remember this wall. Now to get over."

About a hundred yards along a wide-spreading tree threw a great branch over the top of the wall, and towards this Tinker made his way. From the worn appearance of the branch, where it passed over the top, it looked as though a good many people had gone into the grounds beyond with its assistance. Evidently poachers had found in it a useful friend.

At any rate, Tinker had no difficulty in surmounting the wall with its aid. He swung himself over and dropped to the turf on the other side. Then he saw that he had not been mistaken. Far in the distance through half a mile of trees he could just make out the old Tudor place which he recognised as Yvonne's.

Now he began cautiously to make his way forward. For the first few rods the way was easy, but then he was brought up with a suddenness which took his breath away. He had almost run into a keeper who was leaning against a tree watching the movements of some birds overhead.

Only the utter silence of Tinker's advance saved him from discovery. Even as it was he had barely time to drop to the ground behind a nearby shrub when, through its branches, he saw the keeper turn.

He hesitated as though debating whether to move in one direction or another. If he went as he seemed to intend to it was useless for Tinker to hope to conceal his presence, for the man must pass close to him.

But the Fates were for the lad, for, after a moment's indecision, the keeper turned and made off in the opposite direction. No sooner had his footsteps died away than Tinker was speeding forward like a hare. He travelled as straight as the intervening trees would permit, and at last brought up at the edge of the plantation.

Beyond him lay the lawn, the terraces, and the main house. Around to the right stretched the gardens, while to the left was the kitchen garden, and beyond that several outbuildings.

On the other side of the house, and concealed from view by it, he knew were the stables. From where he lay he could just get a glimpse of a building which, if his memory served him right, was the garage. And the plantation circled round until it was close to it.

Rising, Tinker once more took to the woods and made his way in a roundabout direction until he could see the building which was his objective. He dropped to his hands and knees and crept forward. Nearer and nearer he drew until he was less than ten yards from the rear of it.

Now he could command a clear view of the yard beyond it, and he settled himself to watch. The minutes passed slowly without anything of interest transpiring. Half an hour went by and still not a soul had crossed the yard.

But shortly after his patience was rewarded. The side door of the house opened and a man appeared, followed almost at once by another. Tinker almost shouted as he recognised Alec and Hendricks.

Blake had been right, though Tinker couldn't imagine how he had connected Yvonne with the present case, and guessed she was occupying her place in Surrey. But where Alec and Hendricks were then Yvonne could not be far away. The two men walked on, talking, and turned in the direction of the stables.

Now, strictly speaking, Tinker had fulfilled the purpose on which he had come. Blake's instructions had been plain to the last degree. He was to scout about and endeavour to discover if Yvonne were occupying the place. That had been accomplished, and by right he should now retreat the way he had come.

But in Tinker's mind arose a thought born by the nearness of the garage before him. He knew enough of Blake's methods to know that, in his master's opinion, the motor horse-van had played a very important part in the disappearance of the horse Sunset.

Putting two and two together it was not very difficult for him to follow Blake's reasoning and to see that the detective suspected Yvonne of being behind it. That being so, where would a motor horse-van be kept when not in use? Why most likely in the garage.

And if that were so, then why shouldn't it be in the building just ahead of him. It might be. At any rate, the coast was clear, and a window was set in the rear wall at a tempting height. He would slip across the intervening distance, take a peep through the window, then make his get-away.

With infinite caution he began to move forward, keeping close to the ground and taking advantage of all the cover which offered. At last he reached the base of the last tree, and between him and the garage now lay a bare six feet of gravel.

Rising and straining forward in the attitude of a runner about to hurl himself onwards Tinker looked in every direction. Not a soul was in sight. Taking a long breath he bounded across the intervening space at a bound.

Now he was close to the rear wall of the garage, apparently safe from observation. Directly above was the window which had lured him. Its sill was a bare foot over his head, and by a light spring he drew himself up until his chin was level with the projecting flange of the sill.

Then he peered through the glass. At first he could see little. The interior of the garage was in semi-darkness, but, by pressing his face closer, he was able to overcome the baffling glare of the light on the outside of the window.

As his eyes became accustomed to the gloom he took in the objects which were visible. Over to the right stood a great dark-coloured limousine, directly behind if was a touring-car, also of a dark colour.

To the left was another touring-car of a grey shade, and against the opposite wall a huge bulky affair which at first baffled him. Then, as its lines became more distinct, he saw with a sharp thrill that it was a motor horse-van.

With a surge of triumph he loosened his hold and dropped softly to the ground. Then he bounded back to the cover of the plantation, and began to make his way through in the direction from which he had come.

All the way he was muttering:

"Got it! Got it! The guv'nor will be tickled! And I wasn't spotted by a soul."

How little he dreamed, as he dodged along through the trees, that, in a room high up in the great house, a bronze-haired girl stood at the window, a pair of field-glasses held to her eyes and a smile on her red lips as she followed his cautious progress. And how his confident bearing would have been demolished had he heard her murmur;

"Very well done, Tinker. You move with the caution of a redskin. If I hadn't seen you by accident when you came, I think you would have carried out your spying quite successfully. You are well disguised, but I know the shape of those broad, young shoulders too well to be mistaken.

"So your master is on the trail and already has his suspicions? Now I wonder how even his genius was able to see my hand in this? Was it through the blooms? No, impossible! Was it through the theft of the horse, or was it through the disappearance of the baronet. I am inclined to think it must have been the horse.

"But whatever has been the means he is undoubtedly hot on the trail. I think an immediate move is necessary. What a man he is!"

She turned with a little catch of the breath, and, just as Tinker drew himself up over the boundary wall, Yvonne was already issuing rapid instructions.

TINKER'S arrival at Bishop's Manor was anxiously awaited. The steward and Morris exhibited their anxiety by restless pacing to and fro; the trainer by angry outbursts at his stable lads; Blake by sitting in the steward's office and smoking pipe after pipe of strong tobacco.

At last the lad arrived. As the big car swung up the long, winding drive leading to the manor there was a concerted rush for it. Tinker drew up with a jerk and slipped out quickly.

He made straight for the steward's office, where Blake awaited him. The steward and the manager quickly followed, and just as the lad was starting his report the trainer squeezed in with an apologetic air.

Tinker spoke briefly and to the point. When he had finished Blake looked up.

"You found what I expected you would find, my lad, but you took an unnecessary risk in looking into the garage. If the place was occupied by whom I thought, then my deductions made it practically a certainty that a van would be there."

"But I'm positive I wasn't spotted, guv'nor," broke in the lad eagerly.

"To-night will show," replied Blake, briefly.

"Where is this place?" asked the manager.

Although Tinker had made his report before them, he had reserved any mention of where he had been, and none but Blake had any idea. At the manager's question Blake rose.

"You will know very soon now, Mr. Morris. It is almost six. I had not intended moving until eight, but if you will prepare to leave now we will start. I am inclined to think we shall need to act quickly. It will be dusk, any way, by the time we arrive at our destination."

As the others hurried away to get ready, Tinker approached Blake.

"I am sorry, guv'nor, if I overstepped my orders but it was such a good opportunity I thought it a pity to let it go by."

"It may have been too good an opportunity," replied Blake. "However, don't worry my lad. Only you must never think because one makes an advance and retreat without being challenged, that one has not been seen. Sometimes silence on the part of the enemy is not ignorance, but strategy. I simply maintain that it was a mistake for you to break cover."

"Guv'nor, what kind of a car was Sir Hector's?"

"A grey touring car."

"Well, then, sir, I think I saw it, too."

"What do you mean?"

"There was a grey car in the garage with the others."

"H'm! I shouldn't be surprised if you were right, my lad. At any rate, we shall soon know. Ah, here is the steward in his car! Let us go."

Just then a car appeared from the direction of the stables, and drew up beside Blake's. The latter divided up the party by allotting the trainer and the manager to the steward's car, while he himself drove his own, with Tinker beside him, and Davis, the chauffeur, in the back with Pedro.

In this fashion they started for the village of Horton, Blake in the lead. At Horton the latter turned off and drove on for another mile until he came to a cross-roads. There he drew up, and got out.

A moment later the other car came up, and stopped beside him. After some little discussion the trainer was left in charge of the cars, while Blake, the manager, the steward, Tinker, Pedro, and Davis left the road and struck off through the fields.

Blake had not miscalculated the time of his arrival, for it was already dark. It was no easy matter negotiating the fields and woods in that light, but his former acquaintance with the district served Blake in good stead, while Tinkers experience earlier in the day was invaluable now.

After half an hour's tramp they finally arrived at the high boundary wall, and made their way along until they stood beneath the overhanging branch by which Tinker had gained access to the grounds. The lad went first, and dropped lightly to the other side. Then Blake swung himself over, and lifted Pedro from the chauffeur's arms. The others followed one by one.

Now Tinker took the lead, following as nearly as he could guess the course he had taken before. Half an hour later his guiding proved its correctness, for he came to the edge of the plantation at a spot not far removed from the garage. Beyond loomed the dark bulk of the house, and from end to end there was not the faintest sign of a light.

Blake stepped forward, and for some moments reconnoitred the place in silence. At last he turned to his companions,

"I am afraid we are too late. The lack of lights in the place may be but a blind, but I do not think so. Follow me. There is no further need for any particular caution.

He strode forward as he spoke, taking no particular care to conceal his presence, and, wonderingly, the others followed.

Only Tinker guessed the reason for Blake's supposition, and since, if it were true, it would be due to him, he wisely refrained from making any comment.

Straight across the wide lawn went Blake, and mounted the triple terrace. At the top he turned towards the main entrance, and in a few moments the whole party was standing before it. With a low word to them to be on guard, in case the deserted air of the place was a trap, Blake raised his hand, and let fall the ancient knocker once—twice—thrice.

They could hear the sound reverberating through the interior until it died away in the distance. Then they waited. A full minute went by, and Blake was just raising his hand to knock again, when he heard shuffling footsteps inside.

A moment, later there was the sound of a chain clanking; then the door swung open a bare six inches, to reveal an elderly servitor, holding aloft a candle.

"Who is it?" he asked, in a quavering voice.

"Is your master or mistress at home?" demanded curtly.

"No, sir; they are gone."

"Since when?"

"Since tea this afternoon, sir."

Suddenly the man, who was obviously a butler leaned forward.

"Hexcuse me, sir, but hare you by hany chance Mr. Blake?"

A gasp of surprise went up from those behind Blake, but the only sign he gave was a tightening of the jaw.

"That is my name," he replied grimly. "Why do you ask?"

"Because, sir, before the mistress went she said a Mr. Blake might call. She left a letter for you, sir."

Again the smothered exclamations came from behind Blake.

"In that case, you had better release the chain and admit us, had you not?" he remarked quietly. "If you have any doubts about us, let me call your attention to this gentleman behind me." As he spoke, he indicated the steward. "This gentleman is the steward of Bishop's

Manor, a large estate near here. You may know of it?"

"Ho, yes, sir, I do. I'm sorry, sir, but not knowing who hit might be, I didn't open before. I will do so hat once."

Another rattling of the chain followed, then it dropped, and the door swung wide. The butler gazed in amazement at the assorted party which entered, and cast more than one nervous look at the big bloodhound.

But in response to a gesture from Blake, he set down the candle, and shuffled along to a table half-way down the great hall. From it he took a large, square envelope, which he brought back and handed to Blake.

"That is the letter, sir."

Blake took it with a nod, and murmuring an excuse to his companions, tore it open. He carried it close to the candle, then he read;

"I have a strong idea that before many hours are past you will be here. I cannot guess how you have traced my connection with certain things, but when I saw Tinker this afternoon, disguised and dodging through my plantation with the stealth of a Red Indian, I knew that you were on the trail. It would be interesting to know just what enabled you to suspect me. However, I shall be compelled to leave with my curiosity ungratified. I think it is unnecessary for me to tell you why I do leave before you come. Frankly, I do not wish to see you. I know what you would say—I know what arguments you would use. It would be useless. I am determined to proceed. I hope I may carry out my intentions without again running against you. It makes it harder. Yet, if it must be, it must. Because I am practically running away, I do not acknowledge defeat. I have done that which I intended doing, but only the future can tell if I have succeeded in my purpose. Perhaps my motive would be of interest to you. Study the conditions existing amongst the out-workers of such factories as the Trott Manufacturing Co., and you will find it. In the garage you will find Sir Hector Trott's car; in the stable is the horse, Sunset. Neither have been harmed. In the top room in the tower you will find both Sir Hector and the chauffeur. Since Sunday they have had prison fare, and have been compelled to earn that. I must say that the baronet would never fare very well if he were compelled to exist by the work which his outworkers do. Perhaps he will explain what I mean. By the time you receive this, I shall be crossing the Channel. And I still claim the victory. Au revoir, and a pleasant journey back to London.

"Y."

Blake folded up the letter slowly, and returned it to the envelope. What a strange mixture it was—tender, whimsical, bitter, earnest, and mocking—characteristic of the girl who wrote it. He stuffed it in his pocket, and turned to his companions.

"Davis, if you will make your way to the garage, you will find a grey touring car there. Light the lamps, and prepare it for the road.

"Mr. Morris, if you will take the steward to the stables with you, you will find the missing horse. Doubtless, Mr. Grant (the steward) will recognise him."

"But what does it all mean, Mr. Blake?" asked the factory manager irritably. "You act very mysteriously. You bring us to this place, where you are given a letter; then you calmly tell us where to find certain things which are missing. Where is Sir Hector? That is what I want to know."

Blake's jaws came together with a snap.

"Mr. Morris, let me remind you that I undertook to explain the outrage at your factory, to find the missing horse, Sunset, and to trace Sir Hector Trott and his chauffeur. I did not undertake to explain to you my reasons for every step I took.

"Things are mixed up with this case of which you know nothing, and of which I do not propose to tell you. If Sir Hector wishes to tell you anything, he may. When you return from the stables, I shall have him here."

Morris turned away without another word, and, with the steward, passed out. Davis had already departed. When they had gone, Blake swung sharply, and addressed the butler.

"Do you know anything about those who are in the top tower room?"

A blank look appeared on the man's face.

"The top tower room, sir! No, sir!"

"Very well. Lead me there at once. Make haste. I have the authority in this letter from your mistress."

Any protests the butler may have intended making died under Blake's manner, and, without replying, he picked up the candle and led the way up the broad oaken staircase.

At the top they turned down a long passage to the left, then they went up another staircase. Now they came out upon a landing from which led a narrow spiral flight of steps. Up these the butler climbed until he had passed two doors which opened off and came to a third. Here the steps ended.

"This is the top tower room, sir," he puffed.

Blake said nothing, but stepped forward. Yvonne had not said how he was to get into the room, but a glance showed him he would have no trouble. She had left the key in the door.

Turning it, he pushed open the door, and stepped inside, followed by Tinker, Pedro, and the butler. As he did so, he saw a sight for which he had been half prepared by a mysterious reference in Yvonne's letter.

Sitting on a bench were Sir Hector Trott and his chauffeur. It was evident they thought the intruders were their gaolers, for they were looking up with scowling faces. Sir Hector looked little like the spruce baronet. He was more the edition of a very disgruntled tramp.

Around their waists were two bands of iron, by which they were chained to the wall, and although the chains were long enough to permit perfect freedom of movement, they were not long enough to allow the prisoners to reach the two keys which hung on a nail nearby, and which it was obvious would release them.

In front of each were two small tables on which was a littered array of silk and wire. On the floor lay two half-consumed loaves of bread and a large jug of water. On the bench beside each prisoner were half a dozen very crudely fashioned artificial flowers.

Blake took the whole scene in at a single glance, then reached for the keys. He first released the baronet, then the chauffeur. As Sir Hector rose, he turned to Blake.

"I won't ask you now all that has happened, or how you have traced me here, Mr. Blake," he said. "I want first to get my hands on the people who are responsible for this."

Blake laid a hand on his arm.

"Before you say anything more, Sir Hector, will you give me a word in private? I have something to say to you."

With a puzzled look, the baronet followed Blake out to the small landing at the head of the stairs.

"Listen, Sir Hector," he said, in low, hurried tones. "I suspected you would be angry, and for that reason I did not bring Morris and your steward who accompanied me here.

"The horse is safe in the stable, and they have gone for him. Your

92

car is quite uninjured, and my chauffeur is preparing it now for the road.

"As for the persons who were responsible for this outrage, they have gone and are already crossing the Channel. Are you quite sure you want even Morris to know the truth of this? I don't know the facts, but I can surmise the reason for the silk and wire on those tables in there."

"Surmise!" snorted the baronet. "Do you know what we were compelled to do? Before being given even bread and water we were forced to make six artificial flowers out of that silk and wire. That is what we were compelled to do. Not a meal could we have until we did. Ever since we were brought here we have been at it."

"Then don't you think, on reflection, that is all the more reason for suppressing it?" asked Blake. "Pardon me, Sir Hector, but if that got in the papers, can't you see how the public would regard it?"

"You mean in a ridiculous light?"

"Certainly! The reporters would work it for all it was worth. They would represent it in such a light that to-morrow all London would be laughing."

"By heaven! Mr. Blake, you are right," said the baronet, the cold sweat breaking out on him as he thought of that most effective of all weapons, ridicule. "I see now what you mean. My anger blinded me for the moment. I can't afford to have this get out. I will see that the chauffeur holds his tongue."

"I am sure you will find that the wisest plan, Sir Hector."

"You say the perpetrators have gone?"

"Yes."

"All right! I shall say nothing now, but if in the future I can be revenged on that girl—by the way, who is she?"

Blake shrugged but did not reply.

"She came up twice and lectured me for half an hour about my out-workers, and the prices I paid them. Said she was forcing me to make those blooms in order that I should realise— oh! what's the use, I'm helpless to hit back now, but if I catch her let her look out."

Blake let the baronet talk himself out, confident that he had gained his point. Then he spoke to the others in the room, and, they prepared to descend. Before they did so, Sir Hector; turned to the chauffeur and said curtly:

"Harris, not a word of this to a soul. Do you understand?"

And the man indicated that he did, feeling perhaps that neither of them had cut a very dignified figure in the matter.

In the lower hall they found Morris and the steward. They had found the stallion and Davis was now holding him outside. Then they all prepared to depart, Tinker undertook to ride the horse back to Bishop's Manor, and started off at once.

The rest piled into the grey car and, leaving the butler thinking that some species of madness was afoot, drove on to where the trainer was guarding the other two cars. Then the three cars set off for Bishop's Manor.

After a stop for supper, Blake's car, containing his own party, and Sir Hector's car, containing the manager and the baronet, left for London. On the way, Morris, must have puzzled considerably, for to his surprise the baronet maintained a strict silence respecting his adventures.

At the outskirts of the city they parted company, and on arriving at Baker Street, Blake went straight to the consulting-room. When Tinker came in after a moment, he found his master in a strangely irritable mood, so, with a quiet goodnight he left him with his pipe and his thoughts.

And to whom went the laurels?

Blake solved the mystery and found that for which he searched. Yet Yvonne refused to acknowledge defeat. Had she accomplished her purpose? It is a subject for debate.

But one significant thing occurred the next morning. If it did not have its genesis in Yvonne's action, then it was a strange coincidence. It was after a long night's sleep in his own comfortable bed and when he had finished his morning chocolate, that Sir Hector Trott reached for the telephone which stood on the table beside his bed and called the number of his factory. When he got it he asked for Morris, and to that amazed individual rapped:

"Morris, I want a new schedule of prices prepared for all the out-workers. The present price paid for artificial flowers is ninepence a dozen, isn't it?"

"Yes, sir!" answered the manager.

"Well, I want a standard price of two shillings and sixpence a dozen paid, and let them have all the work they can do. Do you understand clearly?"

"Y-e-s, sir," came back the manager's voice. "But how about our competitors?"

"Hang our competitors," snapped the baronet, and forth-with rang off.

The End.
[34200 words]

A WORD FROM THE SKIPPER.
NEXT WEEK'S PLUMMER v. BLAKE YARN.

I've been storing up a little surprise for you, and that is a story introducing George Marsden Plummer and Sexton Blake, with the plot laid round the present Great War.

It's going to be a wonderful yarn! The first chapter opens out in Germany, in which we see Plummer practically starving in the hands of the enemy. And, curiously enough, all criminal thoughts are brushed aside by his wonderful patriotism.

The chapter dealing with his adventures right in the thick of the fight at Mons is a revelation. It makes one's blood rush a little quicker, and imparts the sparkle of enthusiasm to one's eyes.

"The author really surpasses anything he has yet turned out for the "U. J." and that is saying a great deal, I know. But I'll stake my reputation on the statement that he has never done anything better before.

Then Plummer is wounded, my chums, and is left to die on the battlefield. From that moment events follow in breathless rapidity—how he recovers and secures information of the utmost value to Great Britain—how he is invalided home—and how Sexton Blake and Tinker take up the case. Truly I have never read a yarn more packed with incident.

I cannot tell you any more, my chums, but I think I've told you enough to set your appetite on a very keen edge, eh? I want you all to feel now that you will not be satisfied until you have read it. And, while you are thinking about it, just memorise the title:—
"THE CASE OF THE GERMAN TRADER."

YVONNE IN "THE BOYS' JOURNAL."

Many chums have written to me praising my companion and other paper, "The Boys' Journal," for which very many thanks. But a good many have also remarked that it would greatly improve with those stories of Yvonne out in Australia which were promised by me some time ago.

Well, I certainly do agree with these chaps. It would improve the paper, but, you see, I should have started them long ago, only it just so happened that the author has not the knack of writing with his left hand as well as the right.

He has been so busy during the past months that he has not had time to turn them out. But at last I have received the first of the series from him, and, I can tell you, I'm all impatience to rush it into the paper. It's a fine yarn, wonderfully refreshing, full of adventure, and depicting Yvonne's sweet nature in a masterly fashion; and the action of the story takes place long before the smash came that was responsible for Yvonne's life of vengeance. You remember, you read all about that in "BEYOND THE REACH OF THE LAW."

Now, I can promise all of you that this new Yvonne series will soon be in full swing, and I rely upon UNION JACK chums to taste and see. What I want to make you realise is the fact that "The Boys' Journal" is so different from other books.

You may have been told that the "B J." is "rotten." Don't believe it—just try for yourself! I know what the result will be—you will become a regular reader.

And that's what I want you to be. I want to feel that all my "U. J." chums are "B. J." chums also. I have, since I took over the editorship of "The Boys' Journal" endeavoured to make it a rattling good paper, just the kind I used to like when I was a boy, and of which there are so few to-day.

It is not a snobbish paper—it is not a rag!

In the issue at present on sale you will find some fine chapters of Jack W. Bobin's war serial. I will not tell you what I think of that serial, I will merely remind you that he is the author of our Aubrey Dexter series, and I know that will be sufficient.

Now then, you chaps, rally round your Skipper, and get a copy of this week's "Boys' Journal" at once—One Penny Everywhere.

AN APPEAL.

I want you, dear chums, while the war is raging, to excuse me if I do not reply to some of your letters. I am fearfully short staffed; they've all gone to the front, or joined the Army, you know—and shall, while the war lasts, only reply to those really needing an answer.

I'm sure you will not mind. So, those chums who have very kindly written just lately, stating their views, please don't get huffy at the non-receipt of a reply from me; rest assured I have received your letter, and that it has had every consideration.

AN APPEAL TO YOU FROM SOME OF OUR FAMOUS CRICKETERS.

I gladly give prominence to the following letter, with a firm conviction that you will all give only as Britishers can, according to your means. PLEASE DO NOT SEND ANY MONEY TO ME— ADDRESS IT TO H. R. H. THE PRINCE OF WALES PERSONALLY.

TO THE CRICKET-LOVING PUBLIC.

To the Editor,

"Dear Sir,—We, the undersigned, as cricketers, ask you to accord us the publicity which only your columns can give; in order that we may make a direct appeal to the vast cricket-loving public on behalf of the Prince of Wales' Fund.

"This Fund, which has been called into being by His Royal Highness to meet the countless cases of misery and hardship which must inevitably follow on the heels of War, makes an instinctive and instantaneous appeal to the generosity of the public, and we, as cricketers, know that there is no public so sportsmanlike and so generous as the cricketing crowd.

"As the Prince has truly said, 'this is a time when we all stand by one another.' All of us as a nation are members of a national team.

"We have before us as we write the vision of many a fair English cricket ground packed with eager multitudes.

"We have pleasant memories of seas of faces which, in happier times, have watched us play.

"If only at this moment of trial we could gather in the sums which have been paid as gate-money at cricket matches, those on whom the war has laid a desolating hand would benefit indeed. The wives and families of our Soldiers and Sailors could at least be secure from want.

"It is this thought which has given rise to this particular appeal. We ask all those who have watched us play, and who have cheerfully paid their half-crowns, shillings, and sixpences as gate-money, to step forward and contribute over again their half-crowns, shillings, and sixpences to the Prince's Fund, out of gratitude for the enjoyment the cricket field has given them in the past.

"Let everyone who has followed cricket recall to mind the matches he has witnessed, and enjoyed, and let each one contribute according to the pleasantness of his memories. Then we shall have for those whom the War has robbed not only of happiness, but even of the means of livelihood, a truly royal sum.

"Without any undue spirit of self-importance, we may perhaps say that we have contributed not a little to the interest the public takes in cricket, and, therefore, we make this personal appeal from ourselves to all those who love the game to send whatever they can spare to H.R.H. the Prince of Wales, Buckingham Palace, London, S. W.

Yours faithfully.

J. W. H. T. Douglas.
F. R. Foster.
F. H. Gillingham.
W. G. Grace.
Harris.
T. Hayward.
G. Hirst.
J. B. Hobbs.
G. L. Jessop.
W. Rhodes.
R. H. Spooner.
V. F. Warner.
F. E. Woolley.

THE SKIPPER.

www.ingramcontent.com/pod-product-compliance
Lightning Source LLC
Chambersburg PA
CBHW031853170626
46807CB00004B/1704